John Creasey –

Born in Surrey, England in 1908 into a poor family in which there were nine children, John Creasey grew up to be a true master story teller and international sensation. His more than 600 crime, mystery and thriller titles have now sold 80 million copies in 25 languages. These include many popular series such as *Gideon of Scotland Yard*, *The Toff*, *Dr Palfrey* and *The Baron*.

Creasy wrote under many pseudonyms, explaining that booksellers had complained he totally dominated the 'C' section in stores. They included:

Gordon Ashe, M E Cooke, Norman Deane, Robert Caine Frazer, Patrick Gill, Michael Halliday, Charles Hogarth, Brian Hope, Colin Hughes, Kyle Hunt, Abel Mann, Peter Manton, J J Marric, Richard Martin, Rodney Mattheson, Anthony Morton and *Jeremy York*.

Never one to sit still, Creasey had a strong social conscience, and stood for Parliament several times, along with founding the One Party Alliance which promoted the idea of government by a coalition of the best minds from across the political spectrum.

He also founded the British Crime Writers' Association, which to this day celebrates outstanding crime writing. The Mystery Writers of America bestowed upon him the Edgar Award for best novel and then in 1969 the ultimate Grand Master Award. John Creasey's stories are as compelling today as ever.

THE TOFF SERIES

Double for
the Toff

John Creasey

HOUSE OF
STRATUS

This edition published in 2015 by House of Stratus, an imprint of Stratus Books Ltd., Lisandra House, Fore Street, Looe, Cornwall, PL13 1AD, U.K.
www.houseofstratus.com

Typeset by House of Stratus.

A catalogue record for this book is available from the British Library and the Library of Congress.

ISBN 07551-3556-3
EAN 978-07551-3556-1

Chapter One

The First Appeal

"But he didn't do it," said the woman.

"I'm positive he wouldn't kill a man," declared the girl. "You will try to help him, won't you, Mr. Rollison?"

It would have been easy for the Honourable Richard Rollison, known to so many as the Toff, to promise that he would help, and so soothe and comfort the woman, who was the accused man's mother, as well as the girl, his sweetheart. He could have sent them away easier in their minds if not reassured, made some perfunctory inquiries of the police, and forgotten the whole matter. If the girl had been as ugly as proverbial sin and the mother a hag, however, he would not have promised help and failed to give it. As it was, the girl was attractive enough to make him want to help her, in spite of rather too heavy make-up, and the mother sufficiently forthright for him to think that her faith in her son might be justified.

He knew nothing of the women, except their names: Mrs. Benning and Isobel Cole. They had arrived at his house in Mayfair in a taxi, and on arrival at his top-floor flat had been a little on edge and embarrassed; and beneath all this, desperately frightened. Within minutes of being greeted in his large room, their embarrassment had vanished. Now they sat in front of Rollison's large, figured walnut desk, facing him. Each was sitting on the edge of her chair, each eyeing him with great intentness, as if he could save her man. The girl was dark-haired, blue-eyed, comely – or, in modern parlance, she was easy on the eye, and her statistics were undeniably vital. Her hands were clasped in her lap, and the way she sat, absolutely upright, made it obvious that she was terribly upset. She wasn't really young – in the middle twenties, perhaps – she wore a linen two-piece suit, obviously bought from a low-price departmental store, and a little too "smart" and a little too loud a red. The older woman was smaller, much bigger at the bosom, yet with thinner features, a small and pointed nose, and thick grey hair. She wore her Sunday best: a navy blue suit and a white silk blouse, spotless and immaculate.

"You must help Bob," the mother said, pleading. "He's all I've got left."

She was not near tears. She did not appear to know how often that kind of phrase had been used and how hackneyed it seemed. She simply stated a fact: her son was all she had left. That stirred both compassion and curiosity in Rollison, who sat looking very grave – no other expression would have been kind – with his back to his Trophy Wall. He realised that neither of his visitors had noticed that remarkable wall. All they cared about was whether he would help them to prove that Robert Charles Benning was not a murderer, in spite of the evidence piled high against him.

Rollison looked from the mother to the sweetheart, and back again; and then he asked: "Supposing you're both wrong, and that he did kill this girl?"

"But he didn't!" cried Isobel.

"You can't prove what isn't true," said the mother, more calmly. "My boy may have done some silly things—what boys haven't? But he wouldn't have killed this girl, and I don't believe he even knew her well."

"He wouldn't go around with another girl," declared Isobel, taut-voiced. "Everyone who knows him knows that. I would trust him anywhere, with—with anybody."

Her eyes were sparking with her faith and loyalty, and Rollison wasn't surprised when she could sit still no longer. She jumped up and leaned over the desk, pressing against it, very close to him, obviously seeing him as a saviour instead of, simply, a remarkably handsome man.

Rollison glanced at Mrs. Benning, and wondered whether she shared that identical faith. Both felt positive that Bob was no murderer, but it would do no harm to talk to the mother on her own. That would have to come later, if at all.

"What makes you think I might be able to help?" asked Rollison, to ease the tension.

He succeeded, for the girl moved back to her chair and sat down again. He pressed a bell underneath the ledge of the desk – a signal to his man, Jolly, to bring in tea. Neither of the women noticed the movement, and it was the mother who spoke next. The mother was the thinker and the stronger personality of these two; at the moment the girl seemed younger than her years, naïve and simple despite the sophistication her suit and make-up tried to show.

That was why he thought "sweetheart", and not "girl-friend". There was something refreshingly old-fashioned about her.

"We couldn't think of anyone else who might believe us and who might have some influence with the police," Mrs. Benning answered. "Everyone's heard of the Toff, and everyone knows that you're as good a detective as anyone at Scotland Yard." She was looking at him straightly. "You're supposed to be a good man, too."

This was so naïve that it might almost be a kind of simple cunning.

"Mother said she was sure you would help, and she absolutely made me come, although I've almost given up hope," said Isobel. "The police just wouldn't listen to us." She jumped up again. "I've been round to our police station a dozen times, I actually went to Scotland Yard yesterday, but they're all the same. Oh, they're ever so polite, I don't say they're rude, but they simply won't do anything. After all, they want to get the murderer, and they think it's Bob."

"Do you know why they're so sure?"

"They can't be sure!" Isobel cried.

"Isobel, do sit down," ordered Mrs. Benning, and the girl obeyed at once. If Rollison was any judge, the truth about Isobel Cole was that she was suffering very badly from shock. "I know a little about it, Mr. Rollison, but not much—the police don't tell you much if they don't want to," Mrs. Benning went on. "They say that Bob had seen this Fryer girl two or three nights a week for the last month, and that he was with her on the night she was murdered. That's last Monday. It's Thursday now," she added, and closed her eyes. They were glassy bright, and it was easy to believe that she had not slept since Tuesday morning, when her son had been arrested on his way to work. "Everything was quite normal, as far as I was aware. Bob got up on Tuesday morning at a quarter to seven, the same as usual, and an hour later a police car came with some detectives who wanted to search his room. They searched the whole flat, too," she added, bitterly. "I'm not complaining about that. I just say that whatever else he did, my boy would not kill anyone."

"And he wouldn't go about with a girl like *her*," declared Isobel.

Here was an excess of simple innocence, and it was hard to believe it was all natural. But then, Isobel would want to lay it on thick, so as to save her boy friend.

Rollison had read about the murder in the newspapers. It had not rated large headlines, except in one or two editions, for it seemed an ordinary and sordid enough crime. The murdered woman, Marjorie Fryer, had known a dozen boy-friends in a dozen weeks – a butterfly type to whom every man with money in his pocket was an attraction. According to report, she had been promiscuous and attractive. The official story, so far as it had appeared in the papers, was that Bob Benning had murdered her because she had threatened to tell Isobel of the association. Sordid was the obvious word; yet there was nothing remotely sordid about the devotion of these two women.

The door opened; both girl and woman turned, startled, and Jolly brought in a laden silver tray. He was a man of medium height, dressed in black coat, striped trousers, a grey cravat with a single diamond pin. His hair was grey and sparse, brushed to cover as much of his cranium as it could. He had a lined face, appeared to have a tendency towards dyspepsia, and moved with accomplished ease.

"All right, Jolly. I'll pour out," Rollison said, and stood up from his desk. Doing so, he touched the noose of a hempen rope which had once hanged a man and looked as if it could be used for that again; but although it swung to and fro, neither of Bob Benning's champions seemed to notice. As Jolly went out, Rollison picked up the milk-jug. "If I agree to find out the truth, and it proves that you're both wrong, what will you feel about it?" he asked, and in the same breath inquired. "Do you take milk?"

"You can't prove what isn't true," insisted Mrs. Benning. She hesitated, and then seemed to have to force herself to add: "It couldn't be any worse, anyhow. But—"

Isobel seemed to know what she was going to say, and interrupted swiftly: "I don't care what it costs!"

"Isobel, it's no use letting your heart run away with your head," reproved Mrs. Benning. "I was going to say, sir, that we haven't a lot of money, but everyone who reads the papers knows that you're a *professional* detective these days, and we don't need telling that your fee will be high. We can't pay more than a hundred pounds now, but we both have good jobs, and we don't want to skimp on this. How much *will* it cost, though?"

"Money only comes into a case if I'm helping to make or to save money for someone else," Rollison said easily. "Expenses needn't be very high." Usually he referred anyone who talked of fees to Jolly, but that would place this matter on too formal a footing. He proffered a plate of wafer-thin brown bread-and-butter, and, after a moment's hesitation, each of his visitors took a piece. "Now, I want a list of the names and addresses of Bob's friends and acquaintances, details of where he worked, any club he belonged to—anything which might help me to find out where he was on Monday night. Unless you already know," he added, mildly.

"I only wish we did," said Isobel. "I was at my art tutor's—I go to him Mondays, Wednesdays, and Fridays. If it weren't for that I would have been with Bob all the evening. On Mondays I always try to get my washing done; I never see him on Mondays; the other nights he's always waiting for me when I've finished my lesson. I wish I'd never started. I wish—"

"Isobel, it's no use getting hysterical," Mrs. Benning said sharply, and obviously she was more sensitive to over-pleading the case than Isobel. "Mr. Rollison will think he's wasting his time if you go on like that. I thought Bob had gone to the pictures, Mr. Rollison. He said he was going, but he was late in, and I didn't ask him if he'd seen a good picture, so I'm not sure where he was."

"All I know is, he wasn't with Marjorie Fryer," Isobel declared, more calmly. She sat back in her chair as if grimly determined to take the older woman's advice. "Mr. Rollison, I can't tell you how grateful I am, and I'll do anything at all to help."

"*Anything*," echoed Mrs. Benning. "Shall we start making out that list while we're here?"

They had made the list, after much discussion and comparing of notes; there were ten names and addresses, only one of them even remotely familiar to Rollison, as himself or the Toff. The name was of a Captain Maude, whom he knew as a Salvation Army worker. The Army usually judged people well. There were also the details of the furniture factory in Shoreditch where Bob had worked as a carpenter apprentice for three years and a fully qualified carpenter for five; that showed steadiness and dependability. Bob Benning belonged to the Park Street Youth Club, which was Salvation Army sponsored, and he and Isobel spent many of their evenings together there. It was a normal record, and nothing at all suggested that the Bob of this record would ever become a murderer.

But his mother wasn't really sure that he was wholly faithful to Isobel.

Would Isobel's over-earnest manner tend to weary even a young lover?

Would a girl like Marjorie Fryer, who haunted pubs and drinking-clubs frequented by sailors, who made up skilfully, and who had the glitter and appeal of hard-bitten sophistication, have attracted Bob and made him lose his head? Was this simply a case of a young man sowing wild oats and trying to avoid reaping them? There was no reason in the world why it should not be. No mother would admit that her son might be a killer, and Mrs. Benning's determination to come and see Rollison had probably been a last desperate effort to justify her faith.

As he saw them out, Rollison sensed the desperation in the older woman, and in a way he was more anxious for her than for Isobel, who would fall in love again.

It was probably all a waste of time, for the police might have positive proof that Bob Benning was a murderer. At least that should be fairly easy to find out. Rollison pressed the bell under his desk again, and when Jolly came in, said briskly: "Telephone Mr. Grice and tell him I'm on my way to see him, will you? If he's out, find out what time he's expected, but if he's in, let him think I'm really on my way."

"Very good, sir," Jolly said, and picked up the telephone receiver and began to dial Whitehall 1212. He knew, as Rollison did, that if Grice believed that Rollison was on the way he would make time to see him.

Jolly was waiting for a response, and Rollison was filling his cigarette-case from a box on his desk and trying to decide what Isobel Cole did at her lessons, when there was a squeal of brakes out in the street. That was not uncommon for Gresham Terrace lent itself to speed, and many drivers reached the corner before they realised it. But the sound had the customary effect on Rollison, who stepped across to the window to look out. Jolly said into the telephone: "Superintendent Grice, please," as Rollison reached the window.

At first glance he knew that this was no accident.

A small car was drawn up on the other side of the road, front wheels on the pavement. A man was climbing out, and looked as if he were desperately frightened. A motor-cyclist was halfway along the street, swinging round in the road; he had just passed the little car, and would soon be heading back for it.

And the man getting out of it turned and dived towards the porch of a house nearly opposite the Toff's.

The Toff flung up the window, leaned out, saw the gun in the motor-cyclist's hand, and bellowed: *"Drop that gun!"*

At least he might startle the motor-cyclist long enough to make sure that he didn't shoot at the man who now crouched in the doorway.

Chapter Two

The Second Appeal

There was hardly a moment to think.

Rollison saw the motor-cyclist slowing down, and knew that he was preparing to take aim. The small car had covered its driver for a few yards, but now the motor-cyclist had a clear view of the target. Two people were at the far end of the street and a Jaguar was parked nearer the scene of the attack; but that was all.

"Drop that gun!" roared the Toff again.

He saw the motor-cyclist glance up, and the front wheel wobbled. If the man in the doorway had any sense he would run close to the car and save himself now; but he had no sense, and looked as if he were paralysed with fear. Rollison saw all this, and knew that Jolly had put down the receiver without talking to Grice and was crossing the room swiftly.

"Get me something to throw," called Rollison, and heard the flurried movements as the man turned round.

Below, the motor-cycle was almost at a standstill. The driver was no longer looking up, but steadying his machine. The gun was plain to see in his right hand. The two people had stopped, and were staring; nervous. Nothing else moved. Given a second to shoot in, the motor-cyclist could hardly miss his man, and this was no moment to marvel at the fact that cold-blooded murder was being attempted in broad daylight in a Mayfair street.

Then Rollison, arm stretched out behind him, felt something cold and heavy being put into his hand: a glass paper-weight. Bless Jolly! He judged the distance, and shouted again. He saw a yellow flash and heard the sharp report of a shot as he hurled the paper-weight. He missed the motor-cyclist by an inch or two, but the glass smashed on to the hard surface of the road. It seemed to burst, like a hand grenade, and showered the motor-cyclist with tiny pieces of glass. He flung up his right arm to protect his eyes.

"Run for it!" Rollison bellowed to the man in the doorway.

He doubted whether he would be heard; but he was, for the crouching man straightened up and ran straight across the road – not to his car, but towards Rollison's front door. The motor-cyclist had one hand at his face, and the gun was no longer in sight. The engine had still not stopped, and suddenly it roared, as if the driver realised that he dare not stay here. The people at the far end of the street broke into a run now that it was too late either to help or to be injured. A man appeared from a doorway and made for the Jaguar, then stopped to stare at the motor-cyclist, who went by, his machine quivering, and it was impossible to read the registration number. There was just a chance that the man would fall off the machine if his eyes were injured, and Rollison swung round towards the door. It was wide open. So was the front door, leading to the top landing of the house; Jolly had anticipated that he would want to get out in a hurry. Rollison went racing down the stone steps, feet making a staccato tattoo. He felt a draught of air, realised that the front door was open, and reached the ground-floor passage as a tenant from a flat below backed away from the young man who was staggering in from the porch.

The young man had come from the small car.

There was blood on his hands, which were held up in front of him, and some red smears on his forehead. He looked on the point of exhaustion, and was gasping for breath. There was nothing to admire in him, but a great deal of pity.

"Sorry about this," said Rollison to the other tenant. "He's come to see me; I won't be a moment."

He stepped past the startled middle-aged man and the younger one, and stared along the street.

The motor-cyclist had gone.

"Could be as well," Rollison consoled himself, and went towards the car, which was only thirty yards away.

A wing was crumpled against a lamp-post, but not badly damaged. As he had seen from the window, the front wheels had mounted the kerb, but had not gone too far; the lamp-post had prevented that. It was a post-war Morris which looked as if it had been well kept. Inside it was immaculate, with shiny brown leather. Both front windows were down, which was normal enough on a warm summer's day.

Ten yards away from it was all that remained of the paper-weight: a broken nugget of green glass. Splinters of the same colour, beautiful in the open daylight, were spread all about the road and pavement. There were the skid-marks of the car.

"Better get it off the pavement," Rollison called across the road, and the two people who had hurried so belatedly came up and began to exert their strength and importance, and to show how manly they were. The car bumped off the kerb. The men wanted to talk, but Rollison was brusque and almost impolite as he turned and crossed to the open front door of his house.

The middle-aged neighbour, who knew of his reputation, had recovered from the shock, but there was deep feeling in his voice when he said: "I keep hoping you're going to move, Rollison."

"After thirty years?" asked Rollison, reproachfully. "You ought to put a memorial placque over the door. Not hurt, are you?"

"No, I'm all right," the tenant answered. "I suggested that poor chap go up to your flat and have his hands washed. It was just a nasty graze, as far as I can see. What's it all about?"

"I hope he's going to tell me," Rollison said.

The neighbour smiled understandingly, and went off.

Rollison closed the street door and went upstairs. He did not hurry – there were times when speed was essential, and times when it was folly. He went slowly up the stairs, a dozen conflicting thoughts running through his mind. When he reached his landing he found Jolly crossing the lounge hall from the study. Doors led from this hall to the other parts of the flat –the bedrooms, domestic quarters, and bathroom. Jolly was still quite immaculate, as he said: 'I've just tried the Yard again, sir. Mr. Grice won't be in until six o'clock. As it is bound to be reported immediately, I mentioned the incident outside, sir."

"And so showed how anxious we are to co-operate," Rollison said, dryly.

"I have put the young gentleman in the bathroom and given him all facilities for first aid," Jolly went on.

"Nice timing," Rollison said. "Did you leave word that I'd be at the Yard at six?"

"Yes, sir."

"Thanks. Go downstairs and find out if the police are on the spot yet, will you? Tell them that all I know is that there was a crash and the motor-cyclist went haring off. Don't tell them we've a visitor yet—I'd like to find out what it's all about before we play host to policemen. Better put some beer on ice, though."

"I've put six bottles in the refrigerator," Jolly murmured.

"You get better as the years roll by," Rollison said with a grin. "Have a look at the porch of Number 29 and see if you can see a bullet in the wood of the door, or else lying about—only one shot was fired. I heard it. I'd like to see the size of the bullet, and if we could have it for our own Exhibit A, it might be useful."

"I will try to get there before the police arrive," Jolly promised.

"Don't let them catch you putting the bullet in a matchbox."

There was a glint in Jolly's eyes as he said: "Be sure I won't, sir."

Jolly went out, closing the door behind him. Rollison stepped into the passage leading to the bathroom, and heard the sound of water splashing from a tap. He went into a black-and-white bathroom which gleamed and shone. The ceiling was all black and the floor all white, and this may have accounted for the pallor of the "young gentleman's" face. The driver of the small car looked over his shoulder at Rollison, and seemed to be as scared as if the motor-cyclist had stepped into the room. When he saw Rollison, he swung round, and his eyes seemed to blaze.

"Are you Mr. Rollison?"

"Yes."

"The man they call the Toff?"

"Silly of them, isn't it?" remarked Rollison mildly.

He noticed that the other man's knuckles were grazed, doubtless as he had fallen in the porch opposite, but he did not look badly hurt. He also saw that the hands were dripping wet, and as he picked up a towel and handed it to the stranger, he noticed that there was a small jagged tear in the right knee of a pair of grey flannel trousers, and a smaller tear in the sleeve of a puce-coloured jacket. Puce, black, white, and pallor did not really go well together. He understood the gentle irony of Jolly's "young gentleman", for here was a young man in his early twenties, somewhat precious and arty, with over-long coppery-coloured hair and a large bow tie of puce with cream spots. His clothes were obviously made by an expensive tailor, and his education was obviously by one of the public schools, and possibly a university. He was not a person to whom Rollison took an immediate liking, but that did not necessarily mean that nothing was likeable about him.

"You've got to help me!" the young gentleman declared with great intensity. "If you don't they'll kill me."

It was hard not to say: "Why should I stop them?" But there seemed to be real fear in great, browny-grey eyes, fear in the tension of the well-shaped mouth, in the lines at the lips and at the eyes and forehead; this man might be nearer thirty than twenty. He was very thin, too, almost hollow-cheeked. Could he be the starve-in-a-garret type?

"Now take it easy," Rollison said, soothingly. "Tell me what happened and what it's all about."

"Will you help me?"

"When I know what the trouble is, I'll tell you."

"But I'm in desperate need. That man nearly killed me. He—he's tried to twice before."

Obviously he had tried once, Rollison thought, and asked mildly: "Why?"

He spoke as he turned and went out of the bathroom, knowing that the other would come hurrying after him. He stepped to the big room where he had entertained Mrs. Benning and Isobel, opened a corner cupboard which was also a cocktail cabinet, and took out whisky. This young man needed a stiffener, and once he had it, would probably be able to talk more coherently.

The young man was in the doorway.

"What—what is that?"

"A whisky will make you feel a lot better."

"Not for me," said the young man. "I don't drink."

"Oh," said Rollison, and felt very slightly foolish. He put the whisky back, rubbed his hands together briskly, took out his cigarette-case and proffered it.

"Not for me, thanks," said the young man. "I don't smoke."

"So you have all the virtues," Rollison remarked, and tried to stifle the rising of prejudice against a man who looked so pale and puny, who scared so easily, and had neither of the ordinary vices. The prejudice was unreasoning, but it existed. "Were you coming to see me?"

"Yes. I—I thought you might help me. I'm scared out of my wits. I—I'm always looking over my shoulder, I can hardly sleep at night. I'm absolutely terrified, I tell you."

At least he seemed absolutely frank.

"How long has this been going on?" Rollison asked.

"For about three weeks."

"Why?"

"If I knew, I could do something about it, couldn't I?" The first hint of courage he had yet shown was in that response. "I just can't imagine why it's happening; that's what I want you to find out."

"Have you asked the police for help?" inquired Rollison.

With one half of his mind he was interested in this young man whose name he did not yet know; with the other, he was exasperated because he had wanted to concentrate on the troubles of Bob Benning. It would not be easy to concentrate on two such cases at the same time; the police, with their great reservoir of trained men, had every possible advantage of him. He did not take to this visitor, but fear was a common factor in the day's two cases, and this man's fear seemed real.

"Yes," his visitor said. "I've seen the police."

"Didn't they help?"

"They practically told me that I was suffering from delusions," the man answered, bitterly. "One of them actually said that they have five or six people in every week suffering from persecution mania. Oh, it was said very politely, but what they meant was that I should get the hell out of their office and stop wasting their time. The—the devil of it is, there was nothing to justify what I said. Until to-day there hadn't been any open attack. This is the first one, and—and I think it must have been to try to stop me from seeing you. What else *could* it be? The motor-cyclist followed me, as he's followed me for days. I always feared that the time would come when he would attack me, and—well, you saw it with your own eyes, didn't you?"

"I did," Rollison answered. "The police will take you seriously now, all right."

The young man said: "I've got no faith in them at all. They'll make out that it was an accident, or else they'll start probing into things that don't concern them. Mr. Rollison, I can pay you any fee you ask, just name it and I'll pay it, but help me. I must find out what is going on, who wants to kill me, and why. It really is driving me mad, and it's getting worse. Look!" He snatched a cheque-book from his breast pocket, waved it, slapped it down on Rollison's desk, and actually touched the noose of the hangman's rope, without noticing it. Never had that wall, once the greatest pride of the Toff, been treated with such scant respect and so little attention. "I'll make you out a cheque for a thousand pounds, here and now; that will prove how serious I am, won't it? You must help me!"

He took out his pen, a slinky-looking, gold-rimmed one, and leaned forward, to write the cheque. Some time in the next few seconds Rollison had to decide whether to allow him to sign it or not.

And a thousand pounds was a great deal of money. It would go a long way, perhaps all the way, in the defence of Robert Charles Benning, if that young man was ever brought to trial.

Chapter Three

Payment In Advance

The arty young man whose name Rollison did not yet know wrote the cheque swiftly, signed it with a flourish which seemed quite inevitable, thrust it towards the Toff, and cried: "There!"

In that moment he was almost as naïve as Isobel Cole. This could be a kind of cunning, too, but it did not appear to be. The ink was still damp on the cheque, and Rollison could see the wording and the round figure of £1,000. He was a human being. He could almost make out the signature, and was sure that the first name was Cedric, and the whole name looked like Cedric Wright. The ink was purple. The fingers which held the cheque were beautiful and white, long and slender, and the nails were manicured so that they looked as attractive as nails could. The hand was quivering a little, and the cheque seemed to be moved by a gentle breeze.

If he took it, Rollison would be committed to helping this young man. It was useless to tell himself that he could take the cheque, investigate tentatively, and hand it back if he were not satisfied that he could earn the money. There were other factors which could not be ignored apart from the value that this money could have for the two women. Their fear was so different from this man's and yet as great, and to them this amount of money would seem a fortune.

One factor was the apparent truth – and the Toff had long since discovered that all things were suspect until proven – that Cedric Wright-or-whatever-it-was suffered as greatly from fear as the two women, and as young Benning. His money could not help him there, unless it could buy the services of a man who could.

Benning's mother and Isobel had been able to buy those services by their obvious need; not by money.

"For God's sake, don't you understand what I'm offering you?" cried Cedric. "Here's a thousand pounds!"

"So I see," said Rollison, coolly. "Put it back in your pocket. When I've had the opportunity to consider your problem, and if I think I can help you, we can come to terms. What is your name?"

"Dwight."

"Just Dwight?"

"Cedric Dwight."

"I've an appointment at twenty minutes to six," Rollison said, glancing at his electric clock, which pointed to ten minutes to five. "If that gives you time to tell me exactly what has been happening, who you are, what you do for a living, and what might make anyone want to kill you in cold blood, I'll study the facts overnight and in the morning tell you if I can help."

Cedric Dwight said, thinly: "But I might be dead by morning. Why can't you help me now?"

It was a telling question, and he sounded as if he believed that the danger was as acute as that. That conviction could arise from the fact that he was strung up to a pitch of great nervous tension; certainly he had admitted that there had been no open attack on him before.

Was there a way to compromise?

"All right," conceded Rollison. "You can stay here until the morning, by then I'll have been able to make up my mind." He smiled more amiably, in a further effort to reduce the other's tension. "You certainly won't come to any harm here."

For a moment he thought that Cedric Dwight was going to reject that offer; if he did, then there was no problem: he would have to get his help from someone else. But slowly a brighter light showed in the big eyes, as if the significance of the offer slowly dawned on him. He began to smile. He had a good smile, and very white teeth. He became a good-looking young man, if a trifle effeminate. For the first time, Rollison noticed the well-defined marking of his eyebrows and the length of his curling eyelashes.

"May I really stay here? In this flat?"

"Yes."

"Then I'll accept the offer," exclaimed Cedric Dwight. "You'll never know what a relief that is to me."

The odd and almost embarrassing thing was that there were tears in his eyes.

That was the moment when Jolly came upstairs, quite sedately, with a report. There was a police car with three Divisional detectives downstairs, checking what had happened. Two local constables were also there. No one had yet got round to asking where the driver of the small car was, but they were likely to within the next few minutes. Jolly did not make a report on anything else he had found, and nothing in his expression suggested that he had the bullet in his pocket. Rollison went to the telephone and dialled Scotland Yard, while Jolly moved into the domestic quarters, and Dwight stared intently at Rollison, as if at an oracle.

It was odd that anyone should inspire such confidence in a person who did not know him.

It had been as odd that Isobel and Mrs. Benning had felt the same kind of faith.

"Scotland Yard," a girl operator said.

"Is Mr. Grice or Mr. Ribble there?"

"Mr. Ribble is, sir. Who is that?"

"Rollison."

"I'll put you through," the girl said, and a moment later a man answered the call quickly and gruffly, as if the telephone were his enemy and there was no thought of peace between them.

"Ribble speaking."

"Rollison."

"Who—oh—*you*. Thought I told your man six o'clock."

Ribble was not only a rough diamond, but was proud of it; he was determined at all costs to maintain his reputation.

"This is about another little matter," Rollison said. "There was a spot of bother in Gresham Terrace, when someone tried to stop a caller from coming to see me. Your Divisional chaps are outside now. Do you think you could persuade them not to come and see me for the moment?"

Dwight was drawing nearer, his eyes glowing.

"Why should I?" growled Ribble.

"I might be able to get more out of the chap who came to see me than you can," Rollison said. "If the Divisional men question him, and he closes up, neither of us will get anywhere. Please yourself, of course," he added, carelessly, and felt almost sure that Ribble would make the concession.

"Conditionally," rasped Ribble.

"What condition?" inquired Rollison, politely.

"That you keep the person concerned secure in your flat until you've told us what it's all about."

"Granted," agreed Rollison, promptly.

"All right, then. I'll fix it. Good—"

"Don't go!" exclaimed Rollison, and Dwight came towards him, hands raised as if in a kind of prayer to the worker of miracles. "This man is named Dwight, Cedric Dwight, and he has been to see you recently about being followed and his life being in danger. Someone at the Yard suggested that he was suffering from delusions."

"You mean *Dwight*?" gasped Ribble. "That pansy in a purple coat and lavender socks and tie?"

"The description could fit him," agreed Rollison, solemnly.

"If you have anything to do with him, you're nuts," declared Ribble. "I saw him myself, in person. Anyone would think we were wet-nurses around here. Don't tell me anything actually *happened* to him."

"I'll tell you all about it later," Rollison said. "Are you sure that Grice will be back by six?"

"Certain."

"So long," said Rollison.

When he rang off, Cedric Dwight had shifted to a position from which he could look straight into Rollison's eyes. The man was now obviously delighted, for quite unexpectedly he clapped his hands together and waved them above his head. Rollison waited patiently for him to speak.

"You certainly know how to handle the police," Dwight said warmly. "I saw a shocking type there this morning—and yesterday afternoon. Fellow comes from the Midlands, I should say. Got a voice like a band-saw, and hands like hams. Ugh."

Dwight gave an impressive shudder.

"I think I know who you mean," Rollison said. "In fact he's a Londoner."

"Then he must have a father from the north," said Dwight. Now he was talking for the sake of talking, and was obviously much more sure of himself. He turned to look at the Trophy Wall, and appeared to notice what was on it for the first time. He advanced towards it, wonderment in his eyes, one hand outstretched delicately to touch the noose. "Is this a real hangman's rope?"

"Yes."

"Good lord! And this knife …" Dwight touched the handle of a stiletto. "Don't say that was used to kill a man."

"Three men," announced Rollison, flatly.

"And—there's a stain on the blade. Is that—*blood*?"

"The chemical analysis says so."

"Good lord!" breathed Dwight, and his hand roamed from souvenir to souvenir, touching phials of poisons and guns and knuckle-dusters, nylon stockings and locks of hair, feathers and shoe-laces – a dozen more different articles, each of which had played some part in a crime of murder. Then he turned to Rollison, his eyes glowing. "This is as good as the Black Museum at Scotland Yard! Did you solve all these cases?"

"I helped to."

"Well, I'm damned!" exclaimed Dwight, and moved towards Rollison with both hands outstretched, although Rollison made no attempt to take them. "I'll make it *two* thousand pounds if you'll drop everything else and help me," he declared. "Two thousand pounds, in advance."

"We'll wait until morning," Rollison repeated. "What about things for the night? I can probably fit you up, but would you like to telephone home for them?"

"I've a service flat at Apex House," Dwight told him. "I don't run to a manservant." He said that casually and it was almost a contradiction, because Apex House was the most expensive block of service flats in the West End of London, and no flat in it, even the smallest, could be rented for less than nine hundred pounds a year. To this young man, money and water must be very much alike. "If you can lend me a pair of pyjamas and a razor, and your man can get me a tooth-brush, I'll be all right. You've no idea what a relief it is to feel that I'm not going out again. I— good lord! What about my car?"

"If the police haven't moved it, my man will take it round to the garage," Rollison said. He went to the window, where Dwight quickly joined him. Two men in plain-clothes were standing by the side of the modest little car, and talking. Someone had drawn chalk lines round its wheels, and other chalk lines where it had rested on the pavement. Then a police car turned into the street, and Rollison imagined that this was with a message from the yard. "Dwight," he said abruptly.

"Yes."

"What makes you drive about in a secondhand car?"

"Oh, that's easy," Dwight answered, and grinned. "I thought I would escape attention if I were in that kind of a jalopy, instead of my Allard or the Jag. But the swine on the motor-cycle found out what I was up to." His smile faded, and something of the earlier tension returned. "There didn't seem a thing I could keep from him. He knew exactly where I was all the time. I might be at a club, or a pub, or even at a theatre, and be called to the phone and find out that he was there, with vague threats and menaces—just putting the wind up me. I tell you I haven't been able to call my life my own since he started. I was absolutely driven to go to the police, but—"

"Driven by whom?"

"This chap, of course. I was scared into going to them," Dwight said, abruptly. "I felt that I couldn't carry on by myself any longer."

"Are you sure you've no idea why you should be attacked? Why anyone should try to kill you?"

Dwight answered, curtly: "No. I've told you I haven't," but that was obviously not the truth. Rollison told himself that until he had decided what to do, there was no need to probe any deeper. If he did decide to work on Dwight's problem, he could dig out the truth later.

They were still at the window, and the two detectives got into a police car and were driven off. A policeman walked up and down the street, and by craning his neck, Rollison could see that a plain-clothes man was on duty opposite the car, obviously there to make sure that Rollison's guest did not leave. Ribble had carried out his part of the bargain.

The door opened, and Jolly came in, carrying each of London's three evening newspapers on a salver. He put these on the desk, and Rollison knew that there must be some special reason for this: Jolly would not have interrupted unless he was anxious to draw Rollison's attention to something he did not yet know. Rollison walked to the desk as his man went out, while Dwight continued staring at the Trophy Wall, as if it still fascinated him.

Rollison saw a photograph on each of the front pages; the same photograph, of a nice-looking lad with wide-set eyes and a good, strong chin. It did not surprise him to read the caption under the *Globe*:

Robert Charles Benning,
remanded in custody on
a charge of murdering
Marjorie Fryer.

It would be hard to think of two more different-looking young men, or men from more different backgrounds. And Rollison knew that Jolly was throwing his weight on to the side of Benning and the earlier callers.

Chapter Four

Advice From Grice

"Jolly," said Rollison, ten minutes later.

"Yes, sir?" Jolly was in a white apron, and in the small, modern kitchen.

"Mr. Dwight will be staying to dinner and for the night. He wants a tooth-brush and everything else you can think of for the occasion."

Jolly showed neither approval nor disapproval as he said: "Very good, sir."

"And Jolly—"

"Sir?"

"He will need a bath, of course. Tell him in about half an hour that his bath is ready. When he's in the bath, get the keys from his pocket and take an impression of them. See if we can make a duplicate of anything that's obviously a Yale type. He lives at Apex House, and—"

"Apex House keys have an identification mark on them, sir," Jolly informed him. "It is in the form of a mountain top rising out of the clouds. Is it only the front-door key you require?"

"I think I need a new lease of life, to cope with you," Rollison said dryly. "See if anything else is useful. Dwight says that he doesn't know why he was attacked and why he's being harassed, but I don't believe him."

"The obvious possibility is that he is being frightened so as to pay blackmail, sir," remarked Jolly. "I scrutinised the front door and the porch as you instructed, and found no trace of a bullet. Moreover, I was able to stand on the spot where the motor-cycle stopped for a moment—I could see the tyre-marks and where the machine wobbled to a standstill. I had a comprehensive view of the doorway of Number 29, and it would have been impossible to miss the doorway, even if possible to miss the actual target. So—"

"You think the idea is to terrify the young gentleman, and the bullet was a blank?"

"It does seem the obvious possibility, doesn't it?"

"It could," agreed Rollison, musingly. "Never trust the obvious, Jolly. I seem to have said that before."

"You have also made it clear that you agree, sir, that sometimes the obvious is in fact the only possible solution to a problem, and have acted upon that."

"You're too good for me," Rollison conceded sadly. "I must be getting old. So you liked Isobel Cole, too."

"She is a very likeable young lady, sir, but I think my chief concern is for Mrs. Benning."

"I see what you mean. I'd much rather work for Benning than for Dwight, but we'll see what Grice has to say. If I don't hurry I'll be late, and we wouldn't like that, would we?"

Rollison hurried out, passing the spare bedroom where Dwight was now established. He went to the front door and down the stairs, treated the detective on duty to a broad smile, saluted the constable at the far end of the street and, because it was rush hour, did not take his car or a taxi, but walked across Piccadilly, then along the path between Green Park and the Ritz, next into St. James's Place, and thus to Pall Mall and Trafalgar Square. Then it was a matter of striding along Whitehall to Parliament Street and New Scotland Yard. It was pleasantly warm but not too hot, he was in admirable physical condition, and his mind was stimulated by the challenge which faced him: which job should he tackle? And could he wisely take both? There had often been times when a choice had lain before him, but none quite like this. The investigation into the charges against young Benning would probably take a long time, entail much patient work, and force him to call upon the many people whom he knew in the East End. With luck, the Dwight affair could end within twenty-four hours or so. He had only to find that motorcyclist, for instance, and make him talk.

Only!

He might have some luck, though. He had seen both machine and rider, knew exactly what they looked like, and could describe them. The other two people who had seen the machine had only glimpsed it from some distance away; it was almost certain that they would give differing descriptions. These thoughts were chasing one another through Rollison's mind as he walked, a head taller than most of the people among the crowds thronging the pavements and standing with irked patience at the bus stops, or swarming towards the underground stations. Now and again he stepped into a shop doorway, or into a side street, to try to see if he was being followed. He saw no one and expected no one; it was just his habit to take no chances.

Big Ben stood high and majestic against a cloudless, pale blue sky. A phalanx of scarlet buses was moving slowly from Parliament Square towards Westminster Bridge, and a solid mass of people, some carrying their topcoats, surged across the end of Parliament Street towards the bridge and the river. Rollison turned off in the direction of the Yard and reached the gates as the first chime from Big Ben, heralding six o'clock, rang out above the sounds of traffic and people. When he stepped into the large hall at the top of the steps, a grey-haired sergeant with very red cheeks greeted him with a broad smile.

"Six o'clock on the dot, sir. Mr. Grice said to go straight up."

"Thanks, Jim," Rollison said. "How's your wife's mother?"

"Well, sir, not too good, I'm afraid, but you've got to expect it; she's turned eighty."

"Trying for your wife, though," Rollison said, and went striding towards the stairs, completely oblivious of the fact that his stock had risen several places in the eyes of the sergeant and two elderly constables also on duty.

Rollison did not take the lift, but found his way along pale, severe-looking passages towards the Criminal Investigation Department

Building, and then to Grice's room, which overlooked the Embankment and the inevitable stream of traffic. The sun glistening on the Thames greeted Rollison as he opened the door on Grice's "Come in." Grice was getting up from his desk, a tall, broad man who looked rather thin, was dressed in brown, had brown hair flecked with grey, and a sallow skin. The skin at the high bridge of his nose was almost white, and looked as if it were stretched taut. This gave Grice a severe appearance; as did the rather tight lines at the corners of his mouth. He could be severe; he could be the kindliest of men. Just now he looked as if he were tolerantly amused. He shook hands with Rollison, ushered him to a chair, and pushed a box of cigarettes across his polished desk; the desk was almost clear of papers, but had three telephones and a dictating machine on it.

"Well, how's the great Toff?" he inquired.

"Reeling," announced Rollison.

"From what?"

"This VIP treatment."

"That's just to let you down lightly. Don't say you've given up smoking?"

"No. Thanks."

Rollison took a cigarette and lit it while studying Grice's face. He had known the other for over twenty years, and there was very little he did not know about Grice's moods, his ability, and his weaknesses. Now he felt sure that he had news which would not please his visitor and, as he was a policeman and the Toff a kind of private competitor, that amused him.

"Dwight is going to be a great disappointment to you," he said.

"Deluded is he?" asked Rollison.

"Yes."

"Sure?"

"Yes."

"By?"

"A kind of persecution mania."

"Since when?"

Grice chuckled.

"Let's leave the monosyllables," he said, and sat on the corner of his desk, a position he liked because it enabled him to look down on his callers; he was a great believer in the simpler forms of psychology. "He was here yesterday morning and again this morning. The first time he was so convincing that we took him seriously, and he saw Superintendent Morrow." Morrow was an able but earnest officer. "Morrow decided that he ought to check with Dwight's family. He has an aunt and uncle, but he's been an orphan for several years, and lives on his own. The trouble is old-standing, they say. From childhood he has always been frightened of the dark. He imagines shadowy creatures in dark passages, and that kind of delusion. It's so frequent these days that it's almost normal. And if that doesn't satisfy you," went on Grice firmly, "I checked with his family doctor. The doctor knows nothing about this particular delusion, but he does know that there is a history of nervous ailments and tensions—hysteria as a child, too. I could give you chapter and verse, but I don't think you'll want it."

"Not for a moment," agreed Rollison, as if truly humbled. "Never be surprised at what's round the next corner, eh? How rich is young Dwight?"

"Very."

"Sure?"

"By normal standards, yes. He inherited forty thousand pounds and a business which the family runs for him, and he has a big private income. Did he offer you a large sum to work for him?" asked Grice, and laughed, appreciating this joke to the full. "Money still talks, even to the Toff! But you could be had up for fraud if you accepted this from him."

"Interesting case to take to court," said Rollison, as if earnestly. "We'll have to think about it, Bill. I would say that it's no crime to accept a thousand or even two thousand pounds from a man who honestly believes that you can help him. He's at my flat now, as calm and collected as a millionaire, and safe from all his fears."

"You wait until the lights go out."

Rollison grinned.

"I'll try it, and see. But Bill—"

"Yes?"

"He was chased. Positively. I saw the motor-cyclist. I heard the shot."

"There was no sign of a bullet, the Divisional man checked," said Grice. "Two people who were in the street say that Dwight—they identify him only as the driver of a small car—behaved like a madman because the motor-cycle nearly touched him by cutting in to avoid a dog which ran into the road. The motor-cyclist actually came back, to see if he'd done any damage, and drove off when it was obvious that he hadn't. The so-called shot could have been a back fire."

"Ah," said Rollison, solemnly. "I stand defeated. Jolly couldn't find the bullet, either."

"I know. The Divisional chaps saw him looking for it, and would have stopped him if he'd found anything."

"My, my," said Rollison, as if acutely distressed. "It looks as if both Jolly and I ought to be put out to grass." He smiled into Grice's face, realising that the Yard man believed he had come only to talk about Cedric Dwight and did not yet know of his interest in young Benning. Rollison did not broach the second subject yet; he was too preoccupied with the one fact he knew and no one else did: the motor-cyclist had held a gun. That had not been imagination. Rollison had seen the flash and heard the report, and he was not being deluded. There remained the possibility which Jolly had suggested: that the motor-cyclist's purpose had been simply to frighten Dwight. A blank cartridge could make a realistic noise. But whether he took Dwight's retainer or not, Rollison meant to do all he could to trace the motor-cycle and the rider. He liked to know whether he had been fooled.

"Now how about a drink?" suggested Grice. "I'm still practically T.T., but my wife's out at a hen party to-night, and I'm in no hurry."

He bent down to get whisky and a syphon and glasses out of a cupboard in his desk.

"Cedric's a complete teetotaller," Rollison remarked, very thoughtfully. "Is young Benning, I wonder?"

Grice straightened up, sharply, and the good humour faded from his face.

"What's that?"

"Just a little discourse on teetotallers and their simple ways," said Rollison blandly. "Don't tell me that you're handling the Benning case, too. I know you were mentioned in the evening papers, but I thought it only meant that you were in charge."

Grice was looking at him almost grimly.

"What do you know about Benning?"

"Nice looking. Nice mother. Nice girl-friend."

"That woman's a pest."

"So she said."

"So you've been won over by the two champions of young Benning, have you?" Grice remarked, and obviously did not relish this news at all. He sat down, pushed the two bottles across to Rollison, and lit a cigarette, a thing which he seldom did. "Help yourself, and tell me what you've really come about—Dwight or Benning?"

"I was trying to decide which job to take, and thought I'd find out which you recommended. Naturally," went on Rollison, pouring Scotch carefully, "I was planning to take the one you didn't recommend."

"I shouldn't touch either," Grice said, almost too promptly. "I needn't tell you any more about Dwight—sooner or later you were bound to get stung by a psycho; that isn't surprising. As for young Benning—well, it will be an absolute waste of time. We know he often met Marjorie Fryer. In fact he saw her on Mondays, Wednesdays, and Fridays, when Isobel Cole was at her art classes. There's no doubt that young Benning tried to break the association, no doubt that she blackmailed him a little, too. He'd drawn a hundred pounds out of his Savings Bank, and a lot of the money was in her handbag."

"Sure it was his?"

"Yes. It was covered with very fine sawdust—and he'd been working in his carpenter's workshop that day. He says he didn't give it to her, but—well, we'll find that he lost his head and strangled her.

If he had only given the girl a fright, I would have said that she's asked for it. Except for this one episode, he seems a decent type of chap, but—" Grice, shrugging, became almost fatherly. "You don't need telling that a lot of chaps who were nice enough have been hanged for murder they didn't intend to commit. He's lucky—he'll be out in fifteen years or so, and still a young man."

Rollison echoed: "Lucky? If he's innocent?"

"He isn't. There's no shadow of doubt. I don't mind telling you that his girl-friend and his mother nearly wore me down, they were so persistent, but the evidence is absolutely irrefutable. Benning wanted to break with the Fryer girl, she wouldn't let him, and kept making him pay her by threatening to create a scene with Isobel. It drove him to desperation. His scarf was used. He was seen with the Fryer girl at a pub an hour before she was murdered—about an hour, at all events. Her body was found two minutes' walk away from the pub. There are other things I can't tell you, Rolly. It's the tightest case I've had to handle for a long time, and being sorry for the boy or the woman and the girl don't make any difference at all."

Rollison pondered, remaining silent when Grice broke another habit, and poured himself a tot of whisky. He nearly drowned it with soda-water, sipped, and when Rollison still didn't speak, went on almost testily: "What's the matter? Don't say I've found a way of stopping you from arguing."

Rollison tossed down his drink, and stood up.

"No," he answered briskly. "I've a little defiance left, but not necessarily about this, Bill; you sound right. You are probably right. But I can't get Isobel Cole out of my mind. She came to see me this afternoon, and I promised to do what I could. I know, I know," he hurried on, as Grice looked about to interrupt, "there isn't much I can do. But will you fix it so that I can have a talk with Benning? Just let me see what I make of him myself. That way I'll have an easier conscience, and you'll have proved me wrong out of my own mouth."

He was surprised at the intensity of his desire to see young Benning, and knew that Grice could make an interview possible, or else make sure that it could not take place.

Chapter Five

Talk

Grice did not answer immediately, and did not look away from Rollison, who stood with his back to the window. Big Ben struck the half-hour; he was surprised that he had been here so long. The traffic would be slackening and the buses no longer a phalanx, but a thin red line. He saw the reflection of the glittering wavelets of the Thames in the glass of a photograph of a football team on the wall near Grice's desk. He knew that Grice was silent because he was making up his mind, and that there was nothing he could do to help him decide; only exceptional pressure would make him change once he had decided, and he liked always to be absolutely sure of doing the right thing.

At last he said: "I'll arrange a meeting, but you can't see him alone."

"That's all right," said Rollison, and felt warmly grateful to the Yard man, who now brushed his hand over his forehead, as if he were too hot. "When's the best time, Bill?"

"Now."

"Eh?"

"He's here at the Yard," Grice told him. "He hasn't been sent to Brixton on remand yet." He picked up a telephone, and said: "Give me the main waiting-room," paused, and then went on: "Who's with Benning now? ... Yes, hold him until I come down. Thanks." He rang off, and stood up, looking very big and spare-boned. "Just in time," he said. "He would have been on his way to Brixton in five minutes."

They went out, walking fast, but without hurrying, to a room several passages away. Outside a door stood a constable in uniform; he moved aside and saluted. Just inside was another room with a door leading to it, and a curious window in the door-panel. This was made of glass through which one could see from this side, but which looked opaque from the other. Rollison joined Grice near it, and saw another constable, a plain-clothes man, and a young man all standing quite close together. The young man's profile was towards Rollison; at least he had a good chin. His nose was short, and he had a rather rugged look.

Grice opened the door.

Young Benning looked round swiftly, obviously very much on edge. He was pale but for spots of colour on his cheeks, and had very clear brown eyes – scared eyes. His brown hair was ruffled and unruly. When he ran his hand over his chin, his fingers were unsteady; but his gaze was direct enough. He looked at Grice, not at Rollison, and waited for some comment.

"Wait outside, Mr. Forbes, will you?" Grice said to the plain-clothes man. "You too, constable."

They went out as Benning turned to Rollison. He frowned, as if half recognising the visitor. His jaw was set, as if he were determinedly fighting to keep his composure. That was probably typical of the family and of Isobel, too; all three ran true to type.

"Hallo, Benning," Grice cried, and might have been speaking to a friend. "I've brought Mr. Rollison along. He wants a word with you."

Benning seemed to ask: "Where have I seen that face before?" but he didn't speak. He wasn't sullen, simply on the defensive, and probably afraid of saying the wrong thing. It was easy to understand Isobel Cole falling in love with him. They had the same kind of simplicity, as well as the same kind of background, but many a youth of his kind had been spoiled, if not ruined, by the Marjorie Fryers of the world.

Rollison smiled, and greeted: "Hallo, Bob. Your mother and Isobel Cole asked me if I could help, and the police have given me a chance to try. If you didn't kill this girl, the police won't hesitate to try to find out who did."

Benning said: "They take it for granted that I did."

"Did you?"

"I've told them a dozen times—no."

"Did you see her that evening?"

"Yes, I saw her. I've told them I saw her. We met at the Rose and Crown. I went in there to see if a friend of mine was having a drink, but he wasn't. She was there, and wouldn't leave me alone. She followed me when I left, but I dodged her, and I didn't see her again. I simply didn't kill her, and no one can prove that I did."

He talked well, and had a pleasant voice, lacking the overtone of Cockney which characterised his mother's speaking voice. It was more like the girl's. Modern education was beating down the barriers of accent and dialect; and modern education, added to some natural quality, gave this youth a surprising poise. There was strength of character in him, and there seemed a sense of resignation, as well as the fear which showed in his honest-looking brown eyes.

"Did you know her well?" Rollison asked.

"I'd met her at the Rose and Crown and at a club I belonged to, and she was always pestering me, but we weren't *friends*, if that's what you mean. We weren't anything to each other, either. When we first met she asked me to buy her a drink, and, like a fool, I did. After that she kept saying that if I didn't help her she would tell Isobel that we were having an *affaire*. She tried to blackmail me, in other words."

"Did you pay blackmail?"

"No, I didn't. I bought her a drink once or twice and gave her an odd pound to keep her quiet at the pub. I wouldn't have worried about her talking to Isobel; Isobel would have understood."

"Did you tell Isobel or your mother about her?"

"No, I didn't," answered Benning, and a note of desperation crept into his voice. "I didn't see any point in talking for the sake of talking. I didn't think Marjorie Fryer meant anything—she was half drunk most of the time."

"What about the hundred pounds you're supposed to have paid her?"

Benning said roughly: "It's absolute nonsense. I'd got it out to pay a deposit on some furniture; it was going cheap, and my boss would have stored it free. But the money was stolen from me."

"Did you know that some of it—"

"Not that!" Grice interrupted, sharply.

"What did you do after you left the Rose and Crown on Monday?" amended Rollison.

"I went to the pictures," Benning answered. "My pal Joe Maxham wasn't anywhere around, Isobel was at her art class, and I didn't want to go to a pub in case Marjorie turned up again. For the past month she's turned up wherever I've been—haunted me, almost. The pictures was the best place to be sure that she didn't make a nuisance of herself. There was a film I liked at Leicester Square, and I went by underground to Charing Cross and walked to the Odeon. I got back home about twelve o'clock, after having a cup of coffee and a hot dog at a place in Piccadilly. Mum was in bed, so I didn't see her." Benning had been talking with increasing vehemence, and now he was looking at Grice, not at Rollison. "That's the simple truth. I've told this officer and several others six times if I've told them once. They won't believe me, but it's gospel truth."

Rollison found it easy to believe him.

He thought that Grice was ill-at-ease, too.

He made no promises to young Benning, but told him again that if the police had any reason at all to believe that they were wrong, they would check every item of evidence thoroughly. Then he left with Grice. In a few minutes the detective and the constable would take Benning downstairs, and two plain-clothes men would take him in a police car to Brixton, until his case came up again at the East London Police Court. The law and justice were very constant in their habits.

"Well, Bill," Rollison said, mildly, "think he killed that girl?"

"I know the evidence says so."

"It could be fooling you."

"He asked for legal aid, and he'll get it. If it's fooling me, his counsel will find out. Rolly, we've all the evidence needed to convict him," Grice insisted, "and beyond the fact that he's a likeable youngster and you feel that he's telling the truth, there's nothing in his favour. I've met liars before who made the worst lie sound like a page out of the Bible. I don't want to waste my time or your time, and I'll tell you more than I should. Every time the Fryer girl saw Benning she left better off by several pounds. We checked, so that there's no possibility of doubt. She always said she could get money from him, she owed rent and accounts in several shops, and she paid money on account soon after seeing him. What's more, he admits drawing out that money from his Post Office Savings Account. The furniture story is plausible, that's all. Facts are stronger than sentiment, and I've found the facts."

"Ah," said Rollison.

"Don't start behaving as if you'd got sixth sense."

"No," said Rollison, apologetically. "I haven't, Bill, and if I had you'd knock it out of me. Have you looked for any other individual who was at the same place as these two, and from whom Marjorie Fryer could have got the money?"

"Yes—up to a point."

"What point?"

"You know as well as we do that we don't want to pin a crime on an innocent man. He told us his story, and we checked the places he saw this girl last week. No one in any of the pubs saw any man or woman talk to Marjorie Fryer. We didn't check any farther back, because we think it would be a waste of time. He knew the dead girl. She blackmailed him, and he paid her—and he strangled the life out of her."

"It looks like it," said Rollison, sadly. "Pity. Bill, you've been very good, and I won't keep you any longer."

"If you can find a weakness in the case against Benning I'll buy you the best dinner you've had this year," promised Grice.

Rollison's eyes lit up.

"Now there's an incentive! Can I name the place?"

"You can."

"From this moment on I shall dwell on it," said Rollison, and went on very gently: "Because there are times when the evidence can lie, and this is one of the times. That boy didn't kill the girl."

"I don't suppose I shall ever stop you tilting at windmills," Grice said, almost wearily. "Don't run across our chaps too much, will you? I don't want a private war like we've sometimes had before."

"Last thing I want, too," said Rollison, and grinned. "I've two fights on my hands already."

"You mean you're going to take on Dwight?"

"Just far enough to find out how deep his delusions go," said Rollison. "Thanks again, Bill."

He left the Yard a little after a quarter past seven. Parliament Square boasted three private cars, a taxi, and a motor-scooter, and no scarlet bus was in sight. A crowded sight-seeing boat came underneath one of the arches of Westminster Bridge, and the strains of accordion music floated to the Embankment. Two skiffs shot past the steamer like canoes shooting rapids. It was calm and peaceful, London was at rest – and the river drew him, as a magnet; the Thames always did, especially when he had a great deal on his mind. Now he felt that he had more than he could easily cope with. Bravado was not a wise thing. He should have been more non-committal with Grice; now he was committed to fighting these two wars, and it was easy to see that each might prove extremely difficult.

He had seen that motor-cyclist's gun.

He had reached that snap opinion about Benning.

He crossed the wide road and reached the parapet of the Embankment, with the massive structure of the Yard buildings behind him. If Grice were still in his office, and happened to look out, he would see the Toff's back, and would probably be deriding him silently, because he had stuck his neck out so far. Well, why not? Rollison found himself grinning, suddenly filled with a kind of zest. This would be like pulling off a double. The river had answered him, as it so often did. He watched another, smaller river sight-seeing craft heading for the pier at Westminster Bridge, and several smaller ships with great awnings making for the sweeping spans of Waterloo Bridge. It was warmer than it had been in the middle of the afternoon, and on the other side of the river some boys were swimming and diving.

People passed behind him. Traffic passed, now and again there was the rumble of a heavy lorry, but most of the time it was light traffic: cars, cabs, motor-cycles, motor-scooters. One of the things Rollison had to do first was to find out more about that motor-cyclist, and he had probably missed a trick: he should have asked Grice to show him the Rogue's Gallery, so that he could identify the man.

It was too late.

He glanced to the left and saw a young couple, arm in arm, gazing into each other's eyes. The boy was hatless, looked a little untidy, and about Benning's age; but he was ugly. The girl wasn't exactly a picture-postcard beauty, but they looked as if they could not wait to find a secluded corner.

It was a desperately difficult time for Benning and Isobel, who wanted to be together, like these two, Rollison told himself. He must see the mother on her own, then go to see some of his own friends in the East End; they would give him what help he needed.

In five minutes he had made up his mind what to do. He would telephone Jolly, tell him to give Dwight dinner and keep a snack for him when he arrived later. There were telephones at the entrance to the underground station only three minutes' walk away.

He straightened up.

He heard a girl cry out, a kind of stifled exclamation, heard a soft pad of footsteps, and swung round towards his left. He was too late. He felt a buffet on the back of his head, and then a man approaching from the other side bent down, clasping Rollison's legs in his right arm, and heaved him upwards. The attack was too sudden for him to do anything to save himself. He felt the looming of unconsciousness, and then the sickening sense of fear as he hurtled towards the water.

Chapter Six

Fear

Rollison had never known a greater fear.

It was worse because he was only half conscious; the blow on the back of his head had been so severe. He knew that there was little he could do to save himself, and that he would not be able to swim. All these things flashed through his mind as the river seemed to rise up to meet him. He saw the muddy wavelets splashing against the cold stones of the parapet, even saw great white clouds reflected in the water; and then fell flat on his belly. The water closed about him. He gasped at the moment of impact, and took in a great mouthful of the river; it made him want to choke.

He knew that he must not panic; he must simply get to the surface; if he started to struggle he would take in so much water that he would drown himself. He felt the strength of the current, pulling hard at him, and began to strike out with his arm. He struck soft, oozy mud; so he was right at the bottom. God! The river was six or seven feet deep at high tide.

The fear was greatest because he could not make himself obey his own reason. He struggled; and retched, swallowed more water, and felt it going deep into his lungs. He knew the panic which drowning could bring to a man.

He must not struggle.

How could he avoid it? He had to breathe. There was only the thick, muddy water about him, stinging his eyes, thick and noisome on his tongue. Arms straight out, hands together, as in a dive, feet together; then he would reach the surface. But why didn't he? Why did it take so long? The water was like a great weight pressing remorselessly against him. He would have to try to breathe. He could not stay like this any longer. There was an excruciating pain at his chest.

Then suddenly brightness struck painfully at his eyes; he had surfaced. Here was the moment of greatest danger and greatest hope. He was fully conscious now, shock and the fear had done at least that for him. He drew in a deep breath, felt water lapping against his chin, and struck out, not thinking or caring where he was going. The water surged out of his stomach. He felt sick, but was no longer in acute danger. He was swimming enough to keep afloat, although the weight of water in his clothes was so great that he would take a long time to reach the side.

Then he heard voices. He looked round, glimpsing a crowd of people on the parapet, and not far from him, a lifebelt which was secured by a rope to the parapet railings. He struck out for the lifebelt, clutched it, and knew that there was nothing more to fear.

He could rest.

He was beyond thought for a few seconds, except for the vague understanding that people were shouting and telling him that a boat was coming; all he had to do was to hold on. As if he didn't know. The sun struck warm on his face, but his body was cold, and he kept shivering. They were a long time bringing that boat. It was a good thing he had contrived to stay on the surface, for he would have had scant chance if he had depended on help from passers-by. Who could blame them? He began to think, vaguely at first, and to wonder who had attacked him, and why? Had his assailants escaped, or had the crowd caught them? Good Lord! This had happened within view of the windows of the Criminal Investigation Department Building. He had been shanghaied in the shadow of the Yard. If by chance Grice *had* been at the window, he would have seen everything. At least that made the chance of catching his assailants greater.

Unexpectedly, a man with a deep voice spoke just behind him.

"Okay, now. Soon have you out of there."

The boat was near, with two men in it, one of them standing up and balancing precariously in the bows, the other wielding the oars. They had come up to him as silently as the men who had attacked him. The man in the bows moved to one side, knelt down, and held out a hand. Rollison told himself that he could scramble over without much help, and found it more difficult than he had expected. But soon he was sitting with his head in his hands, sick again, his head aching and the memory of fear almost as frightening as fear itself.

They reached a flight of steps at the end of the pier. At least five hundred people must be gathered, watching, and the wooden floor looked as if it would collapse under their weight. For no reason at all, a rugged cheer came from the crowd gathered there and on the parapet and in small boats which were close by. Rollison stepped on to the solid stone, there was another cheer, and he forced himself to grin as he started up, glad that he was able to rest one hand against the wall.

Then, coming to meet him, he saw Grice.

"Did you see what happened?" Rollison inquired.

"Everything," Grice answered.

"Made any arrests yet?"

"We will," Grice said, grimly. "Stop talking until we get across to the Yard."

"I'm all right."

"You don't look it," Grice said. "And we don't want everyone to hear what we're saying. This is worse than a procession!"

Rollison saw that there were crowds lining the road, holding up traffic; and several policemen were clearing a way to allow him and Grice to reach the main gates of the C.I.D. building. The journalists who haunted the Back Room Inspector had gathered just inside, a motley group of individuals, all of whom looked too ordinary to be top-name newspaper men known to the whole nation.

"See who it is?" one man exclaimed.

"*Rollison!*" breathed another.

"The Toff himself in person," cried a third, and he was chortling. "Rollison! How about a statement?"

Rollison managed a grin.

"I'm wet," he announced.

There was a burst of laughter at this simple sally, and the name, the Toff, was taken up. It became a kind of roar. "The Toff," a man said; "The Toff," men echoed; "The Toff," shouted men and women together: *the Toff, the Toff, the Toff!* Cameras flashed, the lights bright even in the day. None of the newspaper men asked more questions, and Rollison realised that they had probably witnessed exactly what had happened, or else they had already talked to eye-witnesses. He saw the constables on duty at the gates staring at him with round-eyed amazement, heard that roaring fade, and went up the stone steps into the hall where earlier he had seen the sergeant and asked after his wife's mother. Soon he was led into a small, shining-white first-aid room on that ground floor.

"No need to fuss," Rollison said. "The sooner I can get into a bathroom and borrow a pair of trousers—"

"You can strip here, and there's a hot shower next door," Grice told him. "I'll fix you up with a raincoat and rug, and we'll drive you back home."

"Thanks. Did you see who tipped me over?"

"Yes, but—"

"We can talk while I get these things off," Rollison said. The first-aid room boasted a small shower in a glass-enclosed cubicle, and there was one large white towel. Other Yard men hovered, the door was always opening and closing, but only Grice was at Rollison's side. Rollison felt almost himself again, but for a slight nausea and a muzzy headache; the relief from fear was the greatest thing. "How many were there?"

"Two—one from each direction."

"That's what fooled me. Recognise them?"

"They were a long way off," Grice said, defensively.

Rollison stepped beneath the shower and turned the hot-water tap on cautiously.

"That's right," he said. "All witnesses are the same: they see something happen in front of their eyes, but you try to make them describe it, and see what results you get. No powers of observation, that's the trouble with people."

Grice said gruffly: "All right, all right. There were the trees in the way, and I wasn't exactly by their side. They were shortish men, both wearing flannels and a blue or black coat, and both wearing rubber-soled shoes. And each," Grice added, in a tone which stopped Rollison from making any comment, "got clean away on a motor-bicycle which had false number-plates."

Rollison jerked his head up, and hot water splashed into his face. He choked, dodged, and demanded: "What?"

"You heard me."

"Dwight was attacked by a man on a motor-cycle which had false plates, remember?" said the Toff, almost happily. "And isn't it a fact that there have been a lot of robberies and hold-ups lately, by men who've escaped on motor-bikes?"

"So you've noticed that?"

"From time to time I prise my eyes open," Rollison said modestly. "Could this be an organised group—and now be after Dwight?"

"I suppose it could be," Grice conceded.

"I think you ought to look into the history of the delusions of Cedric Dwight, don't you?" The Toff spoke light-heartedly because of the greatness of his own relief, and because here was evidence, which the police could not reject, of a possible association between the attack on him and the attack on Dwight. "Remember that there appeared to be an attempt to prevent Dwight from seeing me, and unlikely though it seems, there now appears to be an attempt to prevent me from probing further into the delusions. Perhaps there were delusions, and perhaps someone has been taking advantage of that situation to give Dwight a real reason for being scared out of his wits. Any idea why anyone would try to frighten him?"

"He's wealthy, and his family is wealthy; that's all," Grice answered.

Rollison turned the cold water on, so that he could be fully refreshed, and he took a cold shower which seemed both to take away the headache and to ease the nausea. He towelled vigorously, and was bone dry when he said: "Let me see if I can dig anything else out, Bill. I'll try to have some kind of report by to-morrow."

"I'm not sure that you ought to be allowed to roam about on your own," Grice protested.

"From now on I shall know exactly what to expect," Rollison said, grimly.

"I'll lend you a couple of men to follow you wherever you go, and keep an eye on you," Grice offered, with the glimmer of a smile in his eyes.

"I'll let you know if I feel that I need a bodyguard," Rollison retorted. "How about some trousers?"

"I think I heard someone say they've got a pair," Grice told him.

Ten minutes later, wearing a pair of grey flannels nearly large enough for a man with a fifty-inch waist, and a brown raincoat that was almost too tight for him, Rollison was taken out by a side entrance and handed into a police car, which was driven away by the entrance into Cannon Row. A small crowd of people had gathered, but no one seemed to recognise the Toff. He felt a little more tired than he expected, but told himself that a stiff whisky and a good meal would set him right; all he needed was an hour or two's rest before going to the East End and beginning the quest for the truth about the Marjorie Fryer murder.

And he might pick up some whispers about the motor-cyclist assailants, too; most information filtered through to the East End, and his friends there were legion, all eager to be both his eyes and his ears. He saw that the police had been taken away from Gresham Terrace, as if Grice had given instructions. The driver pulled up outside Number 22, opened Rollison's door, and asked: "All right to get upstairs, sir?"

"Still sound in wind and limb," Rollison said. "Yes, thanks."

"That's a nasty bump you had on the back of your head," the driver observed. "I should take it easy for a day or two, if I were you."

"I will," said Rollison, almost as if he meant it.

He opened the street door and stepped inside. The headache was back, and he fingered the bump gingerly, realising how right the driver had been; much more than the immersion and the scare had affected him. He had better keep off whisky, or it would go to his head, and give him a really bad hangover. He must go steadily, too; no rushing about for a day or two. His assailants had done almost as well as they wanted; had it been a little worse, the injury would have put him *hors de combat*. He smiled at the thought, and then realised that he was feeling hungry – a very good sign indeed.

He reached his own front door.

It did not open.

There was no real reason why it should, and yet Rollison was puzzled. To-night Jolly would surely be on the lookout for him, being very anxious. Moreover, Jolly had a kind of sixth sense which was allied to an ingenious wiring system planned to amplify sounds outside the house. He would have heard the police-car door slam, and almost certainly would have hurried to the front room to make sure who it was. Once he knew, he would open the front door.

That happened very often; yet it didn't happen now.

Rollison took out his keys, and let them rattle, inserted the front-door key, and hesitated only for a moment. There was probably nothing at all to worry about, but he had to make sure. Jolly might be deeply involved in making the impressions of Dwight's keys, for instance.

Rollison turned his key in the lock, pushed the door open a fraction, and then flung it back.

As it swung open, a man whom he had never seen before backed wildly away to dodge the door. In his waving right hand was a shiny leather cosh, the kind of weapon already used on the Toff that night.

Chapter Seven

Cosh-Boy

Rollison saw two things in the same moment: that the man there was young and wiry and powerful; and that although he was taken off his guard, that would last only for a moment. The greatest danger was that someone else might be in the flat.

Rollison jumped forward, stretching out for the other's right wrist. His fingers brushed the cosh as the man tried to wield it; then Rollison gripped the sinewy wrist, and twisted and thrust the arm upwards. If the trick came off, he would have the other helpless – but if the man knew all the tricks of judo, he might throw off the Toff's grip and do him desperate harm.

Rollison heard the man give a little squeal.

There were no footsteps, nothing to suggest that anyone else was here.

For a moment they were locked together; and this man was good – each was near to breaking point. There was determination touched by fear on a hard, leathery, pale face; and greater fear in a pair of very pale grey eyes. Rollison put on extra pressure in a supreme effort, but could not keep it up. If the other didn't give way now—"

The cosh dropped, thudded, and lay against Rollison's foot. The man's tension slackened.

Rollison maintained his grip, with much less effort, and said: "Go back a pace." The man obeyed, and Rollison stepped with him, then kicked the door to and kicked the cosh, which slid along the carpet like a great black slug. There was a moment of silence, during which the fear in the other's eyes dimmed a little, as if he were assessing his chances, and had decided that they were good.

Rollison let him go, gripped his shoulder and swung him round, seized his right wrist again and thrust his arm upwards in a hammerlock; no one could have hoped to break it.

"We're going into the room on the right first," Rollison said, flatly. "Take it one long step at a time. Don't jerk your arm; I'm no good at fixing splints."

The man seemed eager to obey.

He was half a head shorter than the Toff, his hair was cut very short, and he was surprisingly lean for a young man. His scalp showed here and there, very white. His neck was hard and white, too. Rollison urged him forward to the big room. Opposite the door was the desk and the Trophy Wall; and in that wall a small mirror, set so that he could see anyone sitting on the other side. No one appeared in it, and there was only one corner which he could not see. He stepped into the room, still holding the man in that merciless grip, and glanced at the corner to make sure that it was empty.

"There—there's no one else here," the man muttered. "Let me go."

"When I've broken your neck," Rollison said, pleasantly.

He had left Dwight and Jolly here.

He felt alarm rising, worse because his own immediate crisis was over. His head ached and his heart pounded for fear of what he might discover. He did not speak, or tell this man what he would do if he found Jolly injured or dead, but he knew what he would want to do.

An eye for an eye …

He forced the man from room to room, and in each one his fears grew worse. There was no sign of Jolly in the kitchen, the spare room, or his own quarters; and there was no sign of Cedric Dwight. Rollison finished the search and made sure that no one was here, then thrust the man into a closet which had only a small window facing the area at the back. He slammed the door on him, and turned the key in the lock; that gave a moment's breathing space. Rollison drew his hand over his forehead; it came away damp. He went to the kitchen and the back door, and saw that the key wasn't turned in the lock. It was, usually; that was a rule of the flat.

He opened the door on to the platform at the top of the iron staircase.

There was Jolly ...

If it had been anyone else, if it had been at any other time, it would have been funny enough for a laugh. For Jolly was folded up inside the large dustbin, which stood on the platform, and the lid lay near it. A wooden fence hid the dustbin and back door from sight of neighbouring flats and he could not be seen except from this door. His eyes were open, and the fact that he was not moving told Rollison that he was bound by the arms and probably by the legs. Rollison lost a moment in sheer relief, and then said: "All right, Jolly. Give me half a minute."

He saw Jolly's face, the mouth covered with a huge patch of adhesive plaster; his assailants had made a thorough job of that, but had not really hurt him. There remained a big problem: how could he get Jolly out of the dustbin without exerting himself too much? The obvious thing was to turn the bin on one side.

"I'm going to roll this into the kitchen and then lower it," Rollison said. "If anyone comes into the courtyard, we'll have had it."

He heaved at the dustbin, and the edge scraped against the wall; then it began to clatter on the iron platform. The noise was loud enough to be heard in a dozen flats. He turned the big bin on to its bottom edge and rolled it awkwardly over the step of the kitchen door and into the kitchen. Its weight took it away from him, and for a moment it looked as if Jolly would be thrown out, head hard against the handle of the refrigerator. Rollison grabbed, steadied, and slowly lowered it. Now Jolly's head and shoulders were out, and Rollison squatted down, put his hands inside the bin so that he could cup the other's elbows, and draw him out gradually. Jolly's wrists were secured behind his back, and his ankles were tied. So as to make a perfect job, a rope had been tied from wrists to ankles; it was almost impossible for him to move.

Rollison cut the knots.

Jolly stared at him mutely; almost as if he were pleading. There remained the adhesive tape; that had to be taken off with spirit, and there was some in the bathroom. Rollison lifted his man to the bathroom, sat him on the stool, and then took out the bottle of spirit. It was cold on his fingers as it evaporated.

"It'll sting a bit," he said.

Jolly nodded.

After a few minutes Rollison held one corner tightly, and then pulled the tape off; and it came away in one go. He felt Jolly wince, and saw tears of pain fill his eyes, but except for a pale patch round the lips where the adhesive of the plaster had been, there was nothing to show.

"Don't try to talk for a while," Rollison advised, and went out, fetched whisky from the big room, and poured out a tot.

Jolly sipped and savoured it, then drank. Rollison gave him a second nip, and Jolly finished this, but shook his head at the offer of a third. In a voice which was little more than a croak, he said: "I shall be all right, sir."

"You'll be as right as ninepence," Rollison agreed, and began to massage his man's ankles and wrists.

Jolly sat silent and tight lipped, obviously in acute discomfort; but that would not last. Soon a little colour returned to his cheeks, and the glistening which betrayed the tears of pain became dry.

"I caught the man they'd left behind to deal with me," Rollison said. "How many were there?"

"Two, sir," Jolly whispered.

"Did they injure Dwight?"

"I don't think so, sir, but they frightened him."

"They meant to. How did they get in?"

"It—it was my fault entirely, sir," confessed Jolly, and looked as if that were a cause of shame greater than he could bear with equanimity. "They—one of them—represented himself as a detective officer. He was rather like Detective Sergeant Spencer, and the card looked genuine. I wasn't surprised that the police should want to talk to Mr. Dwight, and there was no way of being sure that you would dissuade them, so—I unchained the door. He attacked me immediately."

Rollison said: "There's no need to talk so much."

"I'm perfectly all right now," said Jolly, who looked as if he could faint at any moment. But his voice was a little stronger as he went on: "Dwight knew nothing about it; he was in his room, sir—he had just finished bathing. The men fastened the adhesive plaster almost before I realised what they were doing, and—well, it was obvious that they were expert at trussing."

"Yes, they were," said Rollison, almost musingly. "Then?"

"They heard Mr. Dwight whistling, and went into him. I couldn't see what happened, but I heard a great deal. He was absolutely terrified, sir. *Terrified*. He began to whimper and try to scream, but they made him come out of the room when he was dressed, and took him out the front way. They left the door open. One of them came back in about five minutes and searched the flat exhaustively, sir, but—" Jolly paused, and something like a smile curved the lips which must still feel painful. "I think he missed the soap."

"Soap?"

"With the impression of the keys, sir. I put the soap at the bottom of our stock. I think there's a good chance that it's still there."

Rollison said gratefully: "I told you earlier that you get better and better, Jolly. Did they say anything?"

"Nothing of any significance at all," Jolly assured him.

"I managed to work one of my hands free and was edging towards a telephone when the man noticed me. He tied the cord tighter, and carried me and—er—placed me in the dustbin, sir, to his obvious amusement. At least—" Jolly broke off.

"At least what?"

"The bin had been emptied only this morning," Jolly announced.

Quite suddenly he was smiling, and Rollison was chuckling; for a few moments they were genuinely lighthearted. That mood did not last for long. Jolly began to move about more freely, walked unsteadily to the kitchen and massaged his own sore wrists and ankles. Rollison put on an old suit, returned to the kitchen, turned out the gas, and dished up a casserole which had been cooking throughout the whole of the upheaval. He did not go to the door of the closet where the prisoner was held, and the man did not call out. Jolly insisted on laying the table, but Rollison made his man sit down and eat with him. They ate in a tense and deepening silence. Rollison had never been more preoccupied, and suddenly broke a long silence almost roughly.

"Could we be suffering from delusions too, Jolly?"

"I don't understand you, sir?"

"First a motor-cyclist appears to shoot at Dwight, but although we hear the shot we find no trace of a bullet. Next two men attack me and toss me into the Thames, but—"

Jolly exclaimed: "They did *what*, sir?"

"Hence the trousers you saw me in," Rollison said, and grinned again. "But they did it in full view of the Yard, with a dozen or more people in sight. They'd laid on their escape smartly enough, but it wasn't what it looked like—simply an attempt to kill me. They must have known that there was a good chance that I would be pulled out in time. In the water I didn't think so, but in fact help was there in a few seconds—and I wasn't hit heavily over the head. Was it a fake attempt—meant to scare and not to kill?"

"I see what you mean," agreed Jolly, thoughtfully.

"Now we have this," Rollison went on. "They could have killed you and they could have killed Dwight, but they didn't. What do you get out of all that, Jolly?"

"They are reluctant to commit murder, sir."

"Just want to frighten, not to kill—but they think it's a good idea to create the impression or the illusion that they are killers, and so make the fear greater." Rollison finished a piece of Dorset blue, and pushed his chair back. "Is that how you see it?"

"It certainly does seem possible," Jolly replied noncommittally.

"That's about as far as it goes," Rollison agreed, and took out cigarettes. Jolly smoked very occasionally, and then always small cigars. He was looking very much better, and his voice was almost back to normal. "I wonder how long I ought to leave the johnny in the john," Rollison went on, musingly. "He didn't look the kind to scare easily, but there's nothing like a few hours of solitary confinement to loosen a tongue. I think I'll nip over to Dwight's place first, then go and see Bill Ebbutt, and come back here about eleven o'clock. The chap should be in a mood to talk by then."

"Are you sure you ought to go out again, sir?"

"I'm sure nothing could keep me in, Jolly. I feel as if we're being pushed around with lots of malice, and I don't like it at all."

He stood up from the table and strode to the telephone on his desk; the dining alcove was off the living-room. He dialled a Whitechapel number, and was answered by a man with a wheezy voice, who sounded both breathless and aggrieved.

"Ebbutt's gym," he announced.

"Bill," said Rollison, and momentarily the wheezing stopped. "Rollison here," Rollison went on. "Can you let me have a couple of your brighter boys for a few hours? We've run into trouble, and I don't want to leave Jolly alone while I'm out."

"Pleasure," answered Bill Ebbutt, and there was no longer the slightest note of grievance in his voice. "Anythink I can do to help, that's me. Coupla big boys?"

"Big bright boys, Bill."

"Good as done," declared Ebbutt, wheezing between each word. "I'll send 'em over right away. Better keep a couple in reserve for you, too, from what I 'ear of things." He gave a roar of laughter, and so told the Toff that he had already heard of the incident on the Embankment. "How's my pal Jolly?"

"Bearing up in the face of grave misfortune," Rollison answered, and paused for Ebbutt's gust of laughter; it ended in a choking wheeze. "Bill, there's a little job which you may be able to help with on the quiet, too. Don't say anything to anyone else yet, but think about it so that you'll be primed when I come. Right?"

"Close as a n'oyster, that's me," Ebbutt asserted.

"Thanks. It's about young Benning. Do you know anything about him or the family?"

"Well, as a matter of fact Benning comes to the pub for a drink now and again, I've had him in the gym; nice stance 'e's got, and plenty of what it takes. I would have said 'e was the last chap in the world to do anyone in, but facts is facts, and I know 'e was 'ere with the Fryer girl a couple of weeks ago. What do you want me to find out?"

"All you can about him, his family, and Isobel Cole," Rollison answered.

"Right chew are," said Ebbutt. "That the lot?"

"What do you know about the motor-cycle mob, Bill?"

"Not much," Ebbutt said, "except that they're not any of the regular boys. Don't worry us much, and we don't worry them. I—" He broke off, and a moment later, Rollison heard him say farther away from the mouthpiece: "I'll be seeing you, Mr. Ar. Bit o' trouble in the gym; I'd better go and slap somebody dahn. So long."

Rollison heard the receiver go down, and replaced his own, slowly. Ebbutt was always having bits of trouble in the gym, and this probably meant nothing more than that: but coming at this juncture, it was almost alarming. Rollison saw Jolly looking at him intently, as he stood up.

"Ebbutt will send a couple of men over to keep an eye on things," Rollison said. "I think I'll change my mind and go and see him first. I'll go on to Dwight's place from there. Lock the door and don't let anyone in unless you know who they are for certain."

"You may be *quite* sure of that, sir," Jolly declared, with firm emphasis; and his cheeks turned faintly pink. "May I—"

The telephone bell rang.

"I'll answer," Rollison said, his hand still on the receiver.

He lifted it and announced himself, watching Jolly, and wondering exactly what was in the man's mind. Before he had finished speaking he forgot that, for a man with a Cockney accent cried: "Mr. Ar, Bill Ebbutt's being cut up. Can you come over quick?"

Then the line went dead.

Chapter Eight

The Gym

Bill Ebbutt was a mighty man, both to look at and by repute. He was one of East End's "characters", knew that and played on it, and yet remained one of the most likeable and popular men of Aldgate Pump. He had three loves: his gymnasium and boxing; his wife; and Richard Rollison, whom he had known for very many years. To him, the Toff was always Mr. Ar, and to him, Mr. Ar was the supreme example of the genleman who really knew his way about. They had met when the Toff had been simply the Honourable Richard Rollison, fresh from Cambridge, wearied of the Mayfair smart set, a useful man with his fists, an engaging man with his grin, and a brave man with his love of adventure. They had first been on opposing sides, and then learned to like and respect each other; and now there was nothing that Ebbutt would not do for the Toff, and little if anything that Rollison would not do for Ebbutt.

Ebbutt, moreover, had a large forefinger on the pulse of that peculiar and amorphous district known as "the underworld". That descriptive term gave him and Rollison a great deal of amusement, and yet each acknowledged that there was such a place, although it could not fit into any topographical boundaries. It was like a shifting island in an ever-flowing sea. There was patches of it in the West End and patches in the East; and there were patches also in the most superior suburbs as well as the dockside slums. Ebbutt's particular empire spread far and wide, for he was acknowledged as the best trainer in the pugilistic world of London. Many promising boys reached him, from Hampstead Heath and Highgate, from Putney and Parsons Green. He was a strict trainer, and nothing displeased him more than a man who had competence but no heart. One of the tragedies of his life was that he could never find a heavyweight with a ghost of a chance of taking the world title from across the ocean. He still nursed the desire to do that as a young girl nurses a dream, but his hopes were thinning with his hair. He was very nearly bald, in fact, and that made him look peculiar, for he was a huge man with an enormous punch, tapering off southwards towards small and almost dainty feet, and northwards towards a huge double or treble chin, broad cheekbones, and a small cranium, which looked smaller because of the shiny pate. One small pink ear was very slightly cauliflowered, but his hands were the hands often described as a surgeon's; small, pink, and well kept.

He was in his tiny office, separated from the gymnasium by a small weatherboard partition and a glass door. Beyond the door was the sawdust ring, the punching balls, the vaulting horses – all the impedimenta of a fully equipped gymnasium. There were very few "boys" in to-night, it being so warm; the river and the open fields had called them. But as darkness came they would drift in, some to see Ebbutt, some to train or spar, others to go a few yards towards the corner and the Mile End Road, where Ebbutt's public-house, the Blue Dog, did a roaring trade and paid the expenses of the gym.

There was a smell of sweat and embrocation, of leather and leather polish, of sawdust and of beer. There was a faint haze, too, from the two elderly men who were smoking; no one in training was allowed to smoke while inside the corrugated-iron walls of this sanctuary.

When he had rung off from the Toff, Ebbutt had heard a scuffle in the doorway, leaned his great bulk forward, and seen two men breasting their way in. That was not unusual. There were other gyms and other trainers, and there was a kind of feud between some of them. There were also the "boys" who got steamed or liquored up, and who came simply to throw their weight about, crack a few heads, do a little damage, and then go off in high spirits.

So these two arrivals did not worry Ebbutt, although they puzzled him, for he did not recognise either.

They were biggish men, they were tough, and but for their arrogance and the way they pushed two middle-aged men aside, Ebbutt would have been glad to see them. They looked as if, with training, they could become very useful "boys" indeed, and easy to match for fifty pounds a fight, win or lose. They saw him, and came swaggering across; and that was really the first moment when Ebbutt felt a twinge of alarm. He did not like their confidence nor the sense of purpose which seemed to lie upon them. One of his cronies, a little man who had acted as second to more boxers than he had years, strutted up to the newcomers, thrust out his chest, and stood in front of them. Another, a more cautious man with a matt of grey hair, approached Ebbutt and said out of the corner of his mouth: "Dunno that I likes the look o' this."

"S'all right," Ebbutt said, quietly; and then he saw one of the newcomers dart towards the perky second, who obviously did not expect serious trouble. The three youngsters here for training and a few old stagers were some distance from the spot, none of them prepared for trouble, for there had been no apparent threat of it.

The newcomer smacked his fist into the second's face; and as his arm moved, Ebbutt saw the dull, brassy gleam of knuckle-dusters. The metal smacked sickeningly into the second's jaw.

Ebbutt let out a roar which had no words but the clearest possible meaning. For a large man, he could move with considerable speed, and he was even quicker off the mark than usual. He threw himself forward, knowing that the men would move aside, allow him to pass, and try to trip him up – if he let them have their way. Instead of going straight at them, he swerved to the right, and towards the man with the knuckle-dusters. And instead of using his fists like flails, he threw his whole weight at the man, carrying him bodily backwards. As he struck the floor with the back of his head he would probably lose consciousness, and so leave only one attacker to deal with.

The first part of the stratagem was completely successful. The man crashed down, and Ebbutt, judging skilfully, clutched at the top rope of the ring and kept his balance. Had there been only the two men, he would have been triumphant on that instant; but several others were at the door, and he saw a flurry of fists and feet, sticks and chairs; then a flood of men came surging in, spreading all over the gymnasium, leaping into the ring itself. The few faithfuls there with Ebbutt went down before the onrush, and Ebbutt was so astounded by the weight of the attack that he lost a chance to floor the second of the two men who had attacked him.

He turned.

He saw one of the men with a knife in his hand; and like the Toff had earlier, he felt fear.

He heard shouting, screeching, thumping, the rending noises of splitting canvas and of breaking chairs. He knew that the raiders were here to break the place up. He saw men with hammers and axes hacking at the wall-bars. He knew that when this was over there would be nothing left of his first love, and he felt a furious rage against the perpetrators of this raid. He knew of no one who hated him enough to do this; of no reason for it.

But above all these things was fear of that knife. There it was, poking towards him, with a blade broad at the hilt and narrow at the point, held so that the electric light glinted and scintillated from it. Yet the man holding the knife did not come on at once; he seemed to fear that Ebbutt still had the power to crush him. But others were coming, and Ebbutt knew that some were getting towards his flank, to make sure that he could not escape.

He threw himself at the man with the knife. If the blade swept upwards it would stab deep into his flesh, and he knew that he was near death. But he saw the man flinch, and struck at the knife. His fist met the blade. He felt a searing pain, of flesh and bone; but the weight of his arm carried the other's hand away, and the knife dropped. Ebbutt heard it, drew back, and stamped on it with his great weight. He heard it snap. He saw men leaping towards him, but none of them appeared to be carrying knives; most held sticks and two more knuckle-dusters. He gave a great, bull-like bellow of sound, and flung himself forward again. The blood from his wounded hand splashed into the faces of his attackers, and stained them with scarlet. His weight and the expression on his face combined to drive them back. Two tried wildly to hit him, but he was hardly aware of it. He struck at the man who had used the knife, and saw him fall. He was gasping and wheezing, his mouth was wide open, and now he threw all that he had learned and all that he had taught to the winds, and used his arms like flails. He knew that he could not last long. A man leapt on his back and began to batter him about the head, and the pain of that was almost unbearable, but he did not stop striking out.

Then he heard a sound, for once the most welcome in the world.

A police whistle blew.

Ebbutt heard that through a kind of dynamo whirring in his head. The blast was maintained for a long time, and seemed to come from inside as well as outside the gymnasium. The man on his back jumped off, and the sudden lightening sent Ebbutt staggering; but he did not fall. He stood grasping the rope, swaying, seeing everything as through a mist; a red mist, because of a cut above his right eye. He saw men rushing for the two exits, and several lay on the floor, as if unconscious. He saw great gaping holes in the canvas floor of the ring; the slashed vaulting horses, punctured punch-balls which looked like deflated bladders, splintered wall-bars and splintered chairs. He was breathing more wheezily than ever, and there were moments when he felt as if he would never be able to breathe freely again.

Then he felt a sudden, excruciating pain at his chest; at the left side of his chest.

He cried out.

He did not know whether anyone heard him. The pain was so great that he could not think beyond it. He wanted to scream, but although his mouth was wide open, no sound came. The pain grew worse, worse, worse; it was as if something inside him were bursting and spreading all over him. He was unaware of the pain at his hands now, oblivious of everything except this awful, choking constriction. His legs began to sag. The light began to go dim, and now it was a pale red. He knew that he was falling, and believed that he was dying.

There was a strange silence where there had been uproar. Ebbutt felt as if there was a great stillness also. The pain was easing, but the fear and the despair were still with him. He became aware of a new sound, of a voice, of his wife – Lil. He could see her. She looked very young. He could see her as when she had been young, standing in a circle in the Mile End Road, singing with her high-pitched, pure voice, with the drum beating and the trumpets blowing, the cymbals crashing and the trombone playing. Salvation Army lass and publican had met and fallen in love, and wed – and lived their lives together. She had come almost to hate the pub and the gymnasium, or to say that she did; and as boxing was his first love, the Army was undoubtedly hers. Now she was by his side, her hands upon him, and he knew that she was praying; and she seemed to be praying to him.

There were other sounds.

He could not move, and felt a strange peacefulness still, but he did not want to go. This was the place he loved; this was the woman and these the people. This was his home, created out of nothing. This was his life. He did not want to leave it. He set his teeth, as he had often done in the ring when he had known that the fight was going to be long and tough, and that he might not win.

He heard someone say urgently: "Here's a doctor."

Lil was on her knees beside him. Suddenly, sharp-voiced, she was telling the doctor what to do, and was calling for an ambulance. Ebbutt did not know how long he had been here, he only knew that he would soon be gone.

Then he heard a different and yet familiar voice, and his eyes opened wide for the first time.

Richard Rollison was coming towards him. The Toff. He saw the strain and anxiety on Rollison's face, and tried to smile reassuringly, but that was more than he could do. He heard Rollison say "How is he?" and heard Lil answer: "He's ill, he's terribly ill." Then Rollison was kneeling beside him, Lil standing by his side, and the handsome man from Mayfair was smiling into the face of the ugly man from the East End, saying: "You get better, Bill. I'll get them."

Chapter Nine

Wreckage

Rollison heard men call "Mind your backs," and "Ambulance," and he stood aside from Ebbutt. His right hand rested lightly on Lil Ebbutt's shoulder; he could feel her trembling, and knew that it was because she was suppressing her tears. It was hard to look upon the face of the ex-prize fighter, so drawn, so tinged with blue, so near the mask of death. There was the ugly gash across his right hand, too, and the blood on the floor. Near him, unconscious, was a thick-set man with a knuckle-duster on his right hand.

Rollison put his arm round Lil's shoulder, and moved her to one side. The ambulance men came, with their stretcher, and were brisk and businesslike, untroubled by the weight and bulk of their patient. A doctor came, felt Ebbutt's pulse, seemed to take no more than a perfunctory interest as he stood up and watched the men. The little group was surrounded by dozens of people now, from the pub and from the streets as well as from the gymnasium. Suddenly two helmeted policemen appeared in the doorway, and pushed their way through. But no one spoke, and the silence was strange and uncanny. None of Ebbutt's cronies had ever been at ease with his wife, and now she stood, a pathetic figure in the dusty blue of her uniform and the old-fashioned bonnet with its red trimming and the Salvation Army name proudly at the front.

Suddenly she exclaimed: "Why don't you do something?" she shrugged herself free from Rollison and stepped towards the doctor, who was young, and looked a little bored, perhaps, more fairly, tired. He was a small man, with corn-coloured hair and bright blue eyes which reminded Rollison of Isobel Cole's.

He smiled; and his face was transformed.

"We'll do everything we can, Major, be sure of that." There seemed such warmth in his voice and wisdom in his manner, and he silenced Lil Ebbutt's criticism with those few words. "And we'll pull him through; you don't get rid of a man like your husband very easily."

Lil said, now faltering: "He—he will be all right, won't he?"

"There isn't a thing we won't do," the young doctor promised. "Are you going with the ambulance?"

"Don't try to keep me away," Lil said.

The ambulance men lifted Ebbutt, and Lil returned to Rollison as if to the one man on whom she could rely for help. The crowd made a path. The two policemen, here so belatedly, stood near the door, as if at least they could attend to the obsequies. And whatever the yellow-haired doctor said, Bill Ebbutt looked a dying man.

They carried him out, and Rollison went with Lil to see her man put into the ambulance. Then Lil looked round at the people, mostly her husband's friends, and at the wreckage. Nothing seemed to be in one piece. Here was a large room, which she had seldom entered because she had disapproved of Bill's cronies and his boxing. Her life had been in the streets with the Army band, calling in pubs and clubs with the *War Cry*, serving in the hostels near the docks, doing spells of duty in the West End, among the girls who were lured there by the hope of excitement and the promise of glamour. This was a strange place to her, and yet as she looked upon the wreckage it was obvious that she felt the same kind of love for it that her husband had felt; that it had held her in its thrall, in spite of her apparent disapproval; and sight of it like this hurt her beyond words.

Then the small man who had rushed to the telephone came forward, and broke the silence.

"We'll have it right again by the time Bill comes out've 'orspital," he promised confidently. "No need to worry about that."

"I daresay you will," said Lil, and turned to Rollison again, while the ambulance men tucked Bill in, carefully. "Mr. Rollison," Lil said, "I'm a Christian woman, and I'm not vindictive, but I want those devils caught and punished. If you don't get them, I'll never forgive you."

"I'll get them," Rollison promised, simply.

"Ready, mum," an ambulance man said, and Rollison helped Lil up, beside her Bill.

When the ambulance moved off, Rollison turned to the man who had promised to have the gymnasium put right, and asked: "Did you telephone me, Sam?"

Sam was perky and thin, with bright, beady eyes.

"Yep. And I also knew where Bill kept a police whistle. Had a hell of a job finding it, but as soon as I did, the swine disappeared as if I'd brought an army."

"Did you see them?"

"Every mother's son."

"Recognise them?"

"Most of them were the Razzo boys," Sam declared, and talked of one of the racecourse gangs who would wreck any place – theatre, cinema, mission hall, club, or pub – for a consideration. They had been paid to come here and do this, and the chief problem was to find out who had paid them. The unconscious man might give the police all the answers they wanted, but, if not, he, Rollison, would start searching, even if it meant that he had three jobs to do at the same time. Ebbutt probably had more friends than anyone east of Aldgate Pump; every other man, woman, and child would help, and there would be no hope for the perpetrators of this savage crime.

One of the constables turned towards the door as there was a bustle of movement, and two plain-clothes officers from the Division came hurrying in. These were big men in their thirties, who knew the district well and knew also that Ebbutt was one of its best citizens.

They stopped short when they saw the chaos; but came on again as Rollison put his arm round Lil Ebbutt's waist, and went towards them.

"Know anything about this, Mr. Rollison?"

"I arrived when it was all over."

"Any idea who started it?"

"I think it's your motor-cycle mob," Rollison answered. "Shall we compare notes later?"

"All right."

"There's a job you can do," Rollison said, more calmly than he felt. "Ask the Division to keep an eye on my flat—my man's there on his own."

"I'll fix it," the other promised.

Policemen made a path for Rollison. Men who had often fought and trained in here, rough-looking, tough-looking, bruised, and battered, loud and raucous men who were quite silent; but waves of sympathy and understanding for the Ebbutts came from each one.

It was cool outside, and only a few yards to the back entrance to the Blue Dog. A middle-aged woman was hurrying along the street, for it was still daylight, and she called out: "What's up, Mr. Ar? What's 'appened to Lil?"

Rollison recognised a neighbour who was also in the Army and who would be able to give Lil great comfort when she returned. Now he went up to the flat over the pub, explaining what had happened. There had been a smell of beer and spirits on the ground floor, but the only smell in the flat above was of furniture polish. It was Victorian in its fussiness, but spotlessly clean; as if Lil made sure that every shiny surface had a polish every day.

"Bill will be all right, won't he?" the woman asked.

"Bill won't let us down," Rollison assured her, and smiled as if he really believed it.

And at all costs, he mustn't let Bill down.

There was Robert Benning, his mother and his Isobel, desolate and desperate for help.

There was young Cedric Dwight, with his so-called delusions and his genuine fear – and the fact that he had been taken away and was in the hands of men who might not kill, but could terrify.

And now there was Bill Ebbutt to avenge.

Rollison found himself standing in the yard of the Blue Dog, surrounded by crates of beer, by barrels, by empty bottles, and the smell of beer. There was a buzz of talk from the street, and light blazed both from the pub and from the gymnasium, but no one was in sight here, and he was solitary and very much on his own. He felt almost as if he were the only man in the world, aloof from all the violence and the viciousness which had shown themselves this day, remote and somehow dispassionate in spite of the depth of his feeling. He knew the cause, of course; he was suffering from cumulative shock. There had been hardly a moment to breathe. The tempo had been normal enough until he had visited Grice, but since—

Grice and the attack outside Scotland Yard had started it, shaking him badly. The discovery at the flat had forced a flurry of activity which he had not felt like making, but that had been mild compared with this disaster; and the drive here in a taxi, whose driver had really understood the word "hurry", had been tempestuous.

The man on the motor-cycle who had "shot" at Cedric Dwight might have been one of the two motor-cyclists who had attacked him on the Embankment. Were the two men who had come to see Ebbutt members of the same group? That was one of the first things Rollison had to find out. He could act quickly once that was known. Shadowy figures were moving about the street outside, girls were giggling, a man was singing a tuneless song and breaking off every now and again to say; "Thank you, thank you." Wherever crowds existed there were the itinerant beggars; Ebbutt had drawn such men to him, for he had been as open-handed as a saint.

The street opposite the gymnasium was crowded with at least five hundred people. Policemen were controlling these, and all the cars, bicycles, and motor-cycles in sight.

Motor-cycles.

There was one, propped up near the entrance to the gymnasium, which made him stop and stare. This was an old grey Norton; the machine from which Dwight had been attacked had been grey and old-looking, too. There was a driving-mirror on the handle-bars; there was the same streamlining, and this looked like the same machine. Rollison felt a rush of excitement as he went to it, sat astride it, and felt the springiness of the seat. He studied the registration plate and saw that there were two, fitted into slots – as plates which had to be changed quickly would be. He moved his hands about the controls, looking right and left; no one took any notice of him. He found the self-starter pedal, and rammed his foot on it; the engine started. He eased off the brake and moved towards the crowd, and people made way for him, but no one stopped him. If the owner had been among the crowd, surely he would have realised what was happening by now.

Rollison turned the machine at the first corner, knowing there was a builder's yard just along there. He drove into this, put the motor-cycle into a corrugated-iron shed, and studied the plates. Yes: there were two, and they could be changed at the touch of a switch; a very neat job. Neither registration number would be genuine, of course. He went back to the street. No one appeared to have followed him. Now he hurried, cheered up by the fact that he had found a line of action. Some of the people were coming away from the gymnasium now, the sensation over. More police were about. Here and there men recognised Rollison and called out. The very thin man, tall, melancholy looking, and once a first-class middle-weight, stopped him and said: "Bill will get over it, Mr. Ar, won't 'e?"

"Keep praying, Charlie," Rollison said.

"Was it 'is 'eart?"

"It looked like it to me."

"'Ad a coupla 'ttacks lately," the old boxer said. "'Eknew 'e never ought to exert 'imself. You going after the swine, Mr. Ar?"

"With everything I've got," promised Rollison.

"That's the ticket." The man's eyes brightened. "Anything I can do?"

"Yes," said Rollison, promptly. "Get as many of Bill's boys as possible at the gym by ten o'clock." It was then half-past nine, he knew. "We'll have a council of war."

"*That's* what I like to 'ear," Charlie enthused, and rubbed his hands together briskly. "I'll pass the word, Mr. Ar. That right they got one of the devils?"

"Bill did."

"Trust Bill!" beamed Charlie.

Rollison pushed his way through the thicker crowds at the entrance to the gymnasium. It was nearly dark now, and the lights seemed brighter. Although he had seen all this once before, sign of the wreckage made him stand and stare: nothing had been left whole except the lights which hung from the low ceiling, and the little office where Ebbutt had been when Rollison had telephoned him.

One fear nagged at Rollison: that this attack, and therefore Ebbutt's desperate plight, might be due to him. He did not see how, but the possibility was there, discerned by a kind of sixth sense. Supposing, for instance, the men who had kidnapped Dwight knew that he would go to Ebbutt for help; supposing they had meant to make sure that Ebbutt and his men could give him no help. In short, could this be a kind of decoy raid, to get his mind off Cedric Dwight and his delusions, and on to the problem of finding out who had attacked Ebbutt?

Rollison accepted it as a possibility; that was all.

Then he saw a police surgeon whom he knew slightly bending over the unconscious man whom Ebbutt had attacked. Divisional C.I.D. men were standing by, Sam, and more of Ebbutt's men. There was something in the atmosphere which told of more trouble, and when Rollison saw the inert figure on the boards by the side of the canvas ring, he realised what it was.

This man hadn't moved since he had been here.

Rollison asked, sharply: "Is he dead?"

"Broke his neck," the police surgeon said, standing up slowly. "He must have gone out like a light."

"The hell of it is he's the only hope we had of making someone talk," said Sam, gloomily. "He paid the Razzo boys to join in. A cuppla them told us so. There were two of these so-and-so's, and the other one got away."

Chapter Ten

Council Of War

Not long after Rollison's arrival, the body of the motor-cyclist had been taken away, the police surgeon had gone, and the plain-clothes men were with Rollison and Sam. No one else was in the gymnasium, and no one was likely to come in until the police had left. There was no war between Ebbutt's friends and the police, but a kind of natural wariness. The larger of the two Divisional men was dressed in a well-cut suit of navy blue, and he looked almost as spruce as a matinee idol. He was Detective Inspector Forrest, and on his report would depend what action the police took.

"What do you make of it now, Mr. Rollison?" Forrest was very mild, a man who believed a great deal in outward deference.

"Someone has been storing up trouble for Ebbutt, and came to hand it out," said Rollison. "His heart's a bit dicky, and the exertion caused a collapse. It looks as if he got in just one punch."

"Hmm," said Forrest. "Do you know who's behind it?"

"No."

"Were you working with Ebbutt?" Forrest smiled faintly. "Or was he working with you?"

"I'd telephoned him ten minutes earlier to ask him to get me what information he could about young Bob Benning," Rollison answered, and had the satisfaction of seeing that Forrest was taken completely by surprise.

"*Benning?*"

"That's right."

"Benning wouldn't be involved with the men who do this kind of a shindy," Forrest said, and looked really puzzled. "It's a different line of country altogether."

"I couldn't agree more," said Rollison, "but that was all the help I wanted. Even then, there hadn't been time for Ebbutt to do anything." He knew that Jolly was still alone at the flat, wondering why Ebbutt's men had not arrived. But the police would keep the flat watched all right; later he might even wish that they were not there. "No, I don't see how this raid can be connected with me," he went on, "unless—"

"Ah!"

"I was pushed into the Thames this afternoon," Rollison announced, as if apropos of nothing.

"So I heard," said Forrest.

"Motor-cyclists with double registration plates were involved, and the dead man came here on a grey motor-cycle," Rollison went on. He grinned. "It's in a shed at Mason's Yard in Frith Street; I'd taken it away in case it would help to trace the owner. Will you take over?"

Where a lesser man would have reproached or reproved him for taking the machine away, Forrest simply answered: "Yes "

"Thanks."

"Are you suggesting that smashing up the gymnasium may have been a move to distract your attention?" asked Forrest.

"I simply stated the facts," Rollison answered. "You can draw the conclusions. Inspector, Ebbutt's friends are anxious to start finding out who put the Razzo boys up to this. I think I can hear them outside, raring to go."

"All right," Forrest said, helpfully. "I hope you'll warn them not to take the law into their own hands, Mr. Rollison. There certainly isn't a lot more we can do here. Be a waste of time trying to assess the damage quickly, or to look for clues. How long will this meeting last?"

"Half an hour, probably."

"Let's say we'll want to take over in an hour's time," suggested Forrest, accommodatingly.

"Fine," said Rollison.

There was silence as the two plain-clothes men went out, but soon there came a babble of sound, a rumbling and a thumping. Men streamed into the battered gymnasium, not in twos or threes, but in dozens. It was an astounding crowd. Big men and little men, fat and thin, young and old, men who seemed to have no association one with another, but who were in fact friends of Bill Ebbutt. Every one of these had trained in this gymnasium, been roared at and wheezed at by Ebbutt, had put on the gloves, skipped, swung on those parallel bars, vaulted over the broken horses, punched those deflated balls. Still they streamed in. After reaching fifty, Rollison stopped trying to count, and realised that he and Sam would have to squeeze themselves into a corner, to make more room. Sam was already backing away. He fetched two chairs from Ebbutt's small office, stood up on one, and began to direct the crowd, moving them to parts of the big room which were not crowded. Everyone was strangely subdued, and only a few people spoke, in undertones. Most stared towards the office, and Rollison could be seen above the heads of the tallest. Men in old suits, men in polo sweaters, men in shirt sleeves, men in braces – youngsters in their teens and gaffers in their seventies; all these kept surging in until there was no room for more. But there were impatient calls from outside.

"Keep them quiet aht there!" Sam roared. "Mr. Rollison's going to talk to us."

"Quiet, there!"

"*Quiet!*"

And silence fell.

Rollison stepped on to one of the chairs, knowing more or less what was expected of him, and finding it difficult to put into words. These men shared his feeling for Ebbutt, and the great danger was that they might go too far. One thing was certain: if they found out who was behind this attack, and the men were safe from the police, many among this gathering would take the law into their own hands.

No one called out; there was a rustle of movement as he looked over the assembled heads; that was all. The old man who had stopped Rollison in the street had only just managed to get inside. There must be a hundred or more people still in the street, and he had the impression that they were waiting with bated breath for him to speak.

He could turn them into a mob.

He said, quietly, but clearly: "There's no news about Bill, but a bulletin will be posted up outside whenever one comes in. You'll see to that, Sam, won't you?"

Grey-haired Sam, standing by his side, promised: "Yes. Every hour or so."

"Fine. Now! We all want exactly the same thing," went on Rollison, "and we're certainly going to get it. One of the two men who put Razzo's boys up to this raid is dead. The other escaped. We want to know who it was. *I* want to know who it was," he corrected, and there was a new hardness in his voice. "Once I know, I can fix him. But I won't want him hurt. If he gets hurt, if he should go the way of the other man, then there'll be no one left to talk. And we don't need telling that these two men weren't working for themselves. They were taking orders. We want to know who gave them the orders. And there's good reason to believe that they're connected with the motor-cycle gangs. Keep your eyes open and your ears to the ground for news about that mob."

Men nodded; one or two called: "We will." It could not have been more solemn at a political meeting. And Rollison deliberately kept the temperature down; angry men would do harm, coolly determined men might get the results he wanted.

"There are two other things," Rollison went on. "Bill was going to ask three or four of you to act as a bodyguard for my man Jolly. Anyone here remember Jolly?"

He knew that his man was almost as well known as he was himself; and to these people Jolly was a kind of throwback to an earlier age, yet a man to respect for the things he had done here over the years.

For the first time, many of the men grinned.

"And I've promised to try to help young Bob Benning," Rollison declared. "You know all about the murder of Marjorie Fryer, you know the pubs she and Benning met in. She always said she went to meet him and that he paid her to keep quiet, but it's just possible that someone else paid her, and that he was framed. Don't ask me why. I like the chap, and if he didn't kill her, I'd like to make sure that he's set free."

"Okay here," a few men called.

"It's as simple as that," said Rollison. "Sam, will you select the men who're going to help me and Jolly?"

"Sure," said Sam.

He would do it almost as quickly and effectively as Bill Ebbutt, Rollison knew. He waved his hand and stepped off the chair, feeling a deep sense of anti-climax. He had kept the mood of the crowd quiet all right, and almost wished that he hadn't. They felt as he felt: viciously angry, anxious to hit out and hurt. He was sure that every man present would put everything else aside and work to find the men responsible for Bill Ebbutt's seizure.

How *was* Bill?

There was no change in Ebbutt's condition, Rollison was told at the hospital. It was a coronary thrombosis, and the chances were no more than even.

Rollison spent ten minutes with Lil Ebbutt, and was not surprised to find that she was preparing to stay at the hospital on a night vigil. Three of her Army friends were now with her, and asked if they could help. There was one possibility at the back of Rollison's mind, and he said: "There might be a way."

"Just say the word," a large and heavy woman responded.

"You people go in and out of the pubs a lot, selling the *War Cry*," Rollison remarked. "See if you can find out more about Bob Benning and Marjorie Fryer, will you? Someone's lying, and it would help to know who."

"If we can find out, we will," the woman promised.

Rollison left the hospital about a quarter to eleven. The night was beautiful, and the stars made even the grey roofs and the ugly chimney-pots of this part of London seem soft and attractive. There was a kind of glow in the western sky, as if it would not become really dark to-night. He walked towards the corner, where four of Ebbutt's tougher men, two middle-aged and two young, were waiting by the side of a T-model Ford, painted a beautiful bright blue. As Rollison had no car with him, they were to take him home, and then make sure that there could be no other attack on the flat. Rollison sat next to the driver, and the others crowded into the back. The engine was a little noisy, but remarkably smooth, and the tyres carried the old car along with a pleasing buoyancy. Bill Ebbutt had always said that he would not change it for any car in London.

At Gresham Terrace Rollison saw two shadowy figures near Number 22, but as the driver exclaimed: "Who's that?" he recognised a policeman, the man who always had this beat by night. There was a plain-clothes man on duty too.

"You've got rivals," Rollison said. "What I'd like, if it's all right with you, is two men up in the flat, one in the street, and one at the back for a while."

"Good as done," promised the senior man of the party.

Usually there would have been much leg-pulling and hearty jokes and crude humour. Now there was only a kind of unnatural earnestness. Rollison led the two men upstairs, remembered what had happened when he had last come here, and wondered whether this was the time to question the man locked in the W.C. He felt his heart thump as he reached the top step, for Jolly should open it.

It opened, and Jolly bowed as if to royalty, stood aside, and greeted the two prize-fighters by their names.

"Good evening, sir. Good evening, Mr. Day; good evening, Mr. Wrightson." He was almost absurd with the formality, but it was exactly right for the two men. "I'm very sorry indeed to hear about Mr. Ebbutt. A newspaper man told me," he went on. "I telephoned the Divisional Police Station to inquire." As the two men followed Rollison in to the large room, Jolly added: "There have been no messages, sir, but I wonder if you could spare me a moment to look at the cloakroom door."

"Coming," said Rollison, and took beer and tankards from the corner cupboard. "Help yourselves," he said to Ebbutt's men; at least their reaction to that was normal. He went out with Jolly, knowing that there was nothing wrong with the cloakroom door. "What's on, Jolly?"

"I was concerned because there was no sound from the toilet, sir," said Jolly; and undoubtedly he meant it when he said that he was worried. "So I took precautions, removed the chair which secured the door, and opened it."

Rollison barked: "Don't tell me he's killed himself."

"No, not as drastic as that," said Jolly, "but he has taken some kind of drug. He is unconscious. I left him there, as he was rather heavy. As far as I could judge from the pupils, he has taken morphine. His pupils are pin points, and his pulse very faint. Obviously he meant to make sure that he could not be compelled to talk."

"Well, well," said Rollison, heavily. "Prepared for everything and with everything, aren't they? Anything in his pockets?"

"Nothing at all by which to identify him, sir."

"Jolly," said Rollison, edgily, "I'm beginning to get a little unnerved. These people are very good indeed. Did you make those keys?"

"Yes," Jolly answered, and took three sets out of his pocket. "I was glad to have something to do, sir. But—" He hesitated, and then asked: "Do you think any useful purpose will be served by going to Mr. Dwight's apartments? He isn't likely to be there, is he?"

"In this case I wouldn't be surprised if he isn't dreaming of delusions," Rollison said. He opened the door to the closet and saw the prisoner sitting there, head on one side, mouth slack, looking almost as if he were dead. But there was life in him. "We'll get our boy-friends to move him into the spare bedroom," Rollison went on. "Don't take any chances, Jolly."

"That is exactly what I am anxious to say to you, sir," Jolly riposted.

"If you're warning me to take gun and gas pistol and a little something up my sleeve, you couldn't be more right," said Rollison.

"I have everything laid out," Jolly told him, and Rollison grinned as he went into his bedroom, and smiled broadly when he saw a small gas pistol, an automatic, and two knives fastened to clips, laid out on the bed. The clips were rather like bracelets, and one would fasten round his forearm and the other round his leg. There had been a time when these had seemed melodramatic, but the years had taught them that in times of emergency they were as vital to his safety as the brakes on a car.

"I hope you won't go alone, sir," Jolly said.

"I'm going to take one of Bill's chaps with me," Rollison told him, "but he can come out five minutes after me, and pick me up. I'll be on the corner of Piccadilly and Park Lane."

"Very good, sir," Jolly said.

The simple truth, Rollison knew, was that his man did not want him to go out. That might be partly because he realised that Rollison had endured quite enough for one night; and might be because the speed and gravity of what had happened were unnerving him. It was almost as if someone had made quite sure that he, the Toff, could not work swiftly and well on the most important job.

Only one thing could out-match speed and cunning: obviously, greater speed and cunning.

Rollison left the flat a little after twelve-thirty, had a word with the C.I.D. man still on duty, went to the mews garage where he kept his Rolls-Bentley and a Morris Minor which Jolly used. He took out the small car and parked it near the entrance, against a late emergency, and walked to the corner of Park Lane and Piccadilly. Wrightson came up in the old Ford.

"We'll leave that where we can get at it quickly," Rollison said, and they found a space near a large block of modern flats, which rose towards the starlit sky off Park Lane. This block tapered off towards the top, so that each floor had fewer apartments than the one below. At the top, he knew, there was only one apartment.

This was Apex House, where Cedric Dwight lived in luxury.

Chapter Eleven

Luxury Apartment

"You attract the night porter's attention," Rollison whispered to Percy Wrightson, a middle-weight of considerable achievement. "I'll slip into the lift without him knowing I'm in the building."

"Right," said Wrightson.

He was a man in the middle thirties, good-looking, with smooth features and glossy hair. He did not look like a boxer, for his shoulders were unexpectedly narrow, although his arms and fists carried a remarkable punch. He was in normal times a peace-loving man, and he had a wife and three children.

He went striding into the main entrance hall of Apex House, and Rollison slipped round to a side entrance which, he knew, led into the main hall. The moment he stepped into the building there was luxury. The carpet had a thicker pile than most, the walls were beautifully decorated in gold and pale blue, there were alcoves and easy-chairs and lovers' seats, and at each doorway was an elaborate knocker and equally elaborate bell. Rollison knew that Dwight lived on the fifth floor, and the key gave the number: 55. He heard Wrightson talking in his slow, thoughtful way; he was asking about a woman who, he said, lived in flat 110. There was little doubt that the porter believed that he was a private detective on the hunt for evidence, perhaps for divorce. So the porter concentrated on being cagey. Rollison slipped towards the stairway out of sight, and the thick carpet ensured that his footsteps did not make the slightest sound.

He took the lift from the next floor; it carried him slowly upwards, and stopped as if it were heavily burdened with responsibility. Number 55 was towards the right, which meant that it was one of the better apartments, overlooking Hyde Park. He reached the door, listening intently, for someone might share this flat with Dwight; and neighbours might come out from the flats on either side of 55, or else from those opposite. He heard no sound, which was what he had hoped. He took out the key which Jolly had cut, and it fitted perfectly; Jolly always made sure that he did a first-class job.

Rollison pushed the door open, and stepped into darkness.

Although there was silence, and nothing at all to suggest that anyone else was here, Rollison closed the door without a sound, and stood quite still. His heart was pounding more than he liked, and he had a headache, which could only be partly explained by the bump on the back of his head. He felt much as Jolly: that this was a case where almost every thing could go wrong.

There was still no sound.

He took out a thin, pencil torch and flicked it on; the tiny click seemed very loud. The narrow beam of light shone on to a doorway, and as he moved it round on to photographs of beautiful women, all, surprisingly, not only clad but covered. He recognised film stars of an earlier age, and here and there one whose picture was often in the newspapers to-day.

There were four doors.

Rollison knew the lay-out of these flats, for more than one acquaintance of his lived here, and he had often visited the building. The door to the right led to the main living-rooms, that to the left led to the kitchen, the bathroom, and, beyond, a small servant's bedroom. He went left, shining the torch about. There were cups and saucers on the draining-board, a tray set as if for morning tea, but nothing really unusual. Any servant in a hurry might have left the kitchen like this. Dwight had said that he did not have a personal servant, but used the Apex House service.

Rollison made sure that all the domestic quarters were empty, and then crossed the hall towards the main rooms. There would be a huge drawing-room with a great window overlooking the park; a smaller dining-room which could be approached from the hall, and a large and a small bedroom, with windows overlooking the side street and with a glimpse of the park.

The drawing-room was empty.

Rollison switched on a light, for the first time, and it dazzled him. There were more pictures here, all of women, but these were very different from the photographs outside: each was an oil painting, and each was very lovely. He was startled at seeing a Gainsborough which he had last seen at Sotheby's, and a Millais in his best period. He could not place the other portraits, except to know that each was good.

The furniture was modern, and had the look of having been selected by a professional interior decorator; everything matched perfectly, and nothing except the pictures really had life. The colours were pale blue and gold, which showed a lack of imagination, but no one could reasonably complain. There was a writing bureau, but nothing else where papers or documents might be stored; and even if he found a better place, he did not know what he might find.

He turned towards the passage and to the bedroom opposite; and heard a sound.

He stopped in his tracks.

He listened intently, telling himself that he was not wrong, that he had heard that sound, as of somebody moving stealthily. He had heard such sounds so often that he could not be mistaken; but now there was silence, and it was possible that his nerves were sufficiently ragged to make him imagine noises.

He stepped towards the bedroom door again, and saw that it was ajar. He did not think it had been when he had first seen it, but the light had been poor then, and he could have been mistaken.

Only silence greeted him.

Suddenly he began to whistle lightly, a catchy little modern tune he did not know by name. If anyone was here the whistling would make it seem that he was completely unaware of it.

He opened the door of the spare bedroom and switched on the light. There was a single bed, with scarlet and black drapes and furnishing; a startling room, for the lighting was so designed that it threw up the colours. On these walls were impressionist drawings, all in black and red. It had an unpleasant kind of effect on him, almost as if there was a kind of corruption about anyone who could design that kind of colour scheme and like that kind of picture. Absurd? He turned towards the door of the main room, seeing that it had opened another inch. Now he had to decide whether to surprise whoever was there; or whether to pretend that he had been taken by surprise.

He kept whistling.

Then he moved to the door in a stride and flung it back, as he had the door at his own flat.

The door struck no one, but the light from the great room opposite fell upon a girl.

She had great beauty.

There was no reason why Rollison should be surprised, and yet he was. The girl stood there in a pair of lemon-coloured pyjamas, and looked scared, which was hardly surprising. Not terrified; just scared. She was shorter than the average girl, her hair was like the doctor's at Ebbutt's gymnasium, corn-coloured, beautifully waved, and yet looking quite natural. Her eyes were enormous, and cornflower blue, if this light told the truth. Her throat was bare, but the top button of the pyjama jacket was decorously fastened. Perhaps the fact that she had on no make-up, and that her feet were bare, added to the degree of Rollison's surprise at seeing her. Undoubtedly she was an elfin creature, not only of great beauty, but also of great charm. She reminded him, instantly, of Brigitte Bardot.

Slowly her expression changed. The scared look turned into one of fright. She put her right hand up to her throat, as if protectingly. Her eyes glistened, and she moistened her lips, but made no attempt to speak.

"Hallo," Rollison greeted, and hoped that he sounded much less surprised than he felt. "I thought the flat was empty. Who are you?"

She didn't answer.

He was reminded of Isobel Cole, not because of any similarity in features or in expression, but because of that direct and almost naïve look; of bewilderment and simplicity. That could be a pose, for she had known for some time that someone was in the flat, and might have decided what action she would take.

"Who are you?" Rollison repeated, and smiled as if this were the most normal thing in the world. "Does Cedric know you're here?"

She didn't answer; and the silence began to irk Rollison, partly because he could not understand it. Why didn't she make an attempt to speak? He could understand if she tried and failed, if she only got a tumbling sentence or two out, even if she turned and tried to get away from him and slam the door in his face. But she did none of these things.

Rollison's voice sharpened: "I'm a friend of Mr. Dwight. Does he know you're here?"

At last the girl tried to answer, and he thought that she was saying yes. He jumped to the obvious conclusion; that Cedric Dwight did not live alone, and that was hardly surprising, for money could still buy almost everything, and the credulity of a girl like this would probably make it easier for him to have his triumphs.

"Y-y-yes," she said.

Rollison smiled, trying to be patient, and did not move. If he did, he would probably terrify her.

"Who are you?" he inquired again.

She hesitated, then began to speak, and he saw that she was framing the word "I". She could not get beyond it, and said "I-I-I" some six or seven times. The first shock would have explained her early silence, but surely she could see that he meant her no harm.

Then she blurted out: *"I'm his wife!"*

"Oh, no," thought Rollison, and wished that there was somewhere to sit down. Cedric, married? He had not said that he was a bachelor, had made no claims at all, but – married? It was possible that *"wife"* was euphemistic, but somehow Rollison did not think that. This girl was the wife of Cedric Dwight, or had good reason to believe that she was.

"He forgot to tell me that he was married," Rollison declared, as if that were a reasonable comment for a man supposed to know Cedric Dwight so well.

He stepped forward, and the girl backed away. She not only backed, but darted a glance towards the right; her right – and Rollison's left. That was the moment which carried the warning to him; the moment when he realised that this girl wasn't alone.

Someone was standing close to the wall, ready to jump or strike at him the moment he stepped over the threshold; and the girl was still backing away, as if to lure him on.

Chapter Twelve

Deception?

There was the one obvious possibility here: that this girl was really Cedric's wife, that she had believed that he was away for the night, and had shared her charms with another man. Copped, as Bill Ebbutt would have said. That might explain her expression, the change from the immediate fright to genuine fear. But there were other possibilities, too. Dwight himself might be behind the door, anxious to keep out of the visitor's sight.

Was that possible?

Rollison said: "I won't hurt you, I assure you. I've come to try to help your husband." He took another step forward, and still she backed away. It was dark in the room, except by the open door, and she looked ethereal in that dim light; a shadowy figure with silky hair all brushed with beauty, almost as if she were not real, but painted: like the Millais, with its wistfulness.

He reached the threshold, stepped inside – and took a swift step backwards. The trick worked. A man standing behind the wall leapt at him, but because he moved back, missed. Rollison shot out a foot. The other kicked against it and sprawled headlong, having no chance to save himself. Rollison saw the slug-like blackjack which slid over the carpet and came to rest at this girl's feet.

This might be one of the men who had staged the attack on Ebbutt; that blackjack told its own story. It warned Rollison what was likely to happen in future, too.

The girl had turned and run farther into the room, the man was scrabbling to get to his feet. Rollison simply dropped his right hand to his pocket and took out his automatic; he covered the man, and the scrabbling stopped.

"Don't get up," he ordered. "And don't think I won't shoot." He moved his right hand and switched on the light; it came from a chandelier in the middle of the ceiling, a beautiful one of porcelain, and it was reflected in the heart-shaped mirror which hung over the fireplace, an imitation Adam. "Put on a dressing-gown," he said to the girl. "Then tell me what all this is about."

"He—he was going to kill me!" she exclaimed. She did not even look towards the bed, or the dressing-gown over the foot of it. Instead, she drew nearer Rollison, her great eyes showing not only relief, but also the reflection of her fear. "He told me he'd kill me if I didn't—"

The man on the floor chose that moment to move.

He ignored Rollison's warning, behaving as if he had never heard it. He leapt at the girl. On that instant Rollison knew that if he fired at him, he might hit the girl. It had been done so swiftly and with such cold courage that Rollison had no chance to stop it. And now the man's hands were at the little beauty's throat, and it seemed as if he intended to choke the life out of her – or break her neck.

Rollison had a quick mental image of the "unconscious" man in Bill Ebbutt's gymnasium.

Then he went forward.

The man, with his hands round the girl's throat, was carrying her back towards the bed, and she fetched up against it and fell backwards before Rollison could help. Her assailant seemed quite oblivious of Rollison, was breathing heavily, and seemed intent to kill. Rollison shifted the gun in his hand, held it by the barrel, and brought it down on the back of the other's head.

The man's hold slackened. He gave a little gasp, and then began to slide down. His hands dragged from the tip of the pyjama jacket, dragging it downwards, and for a moment he was held up because his weight was helped by the jacket. Then the fabric tore. He slid to the floor, quite unconscious, while the girl struggled to get upright, with her hands at her throat. She was crying in a curious choking way, as if she could hardly breathe yet had to cry. Rollison reached her and put a hand round her waist, then sat her upright on the side of the bed. She still clutched at her throat. Her mouth was open as she fought for breath; it was that, not crying, which made the peculiar noise.

If Rollison judged her aright, it would be a long time before she was collected enough to talk to him, and it would be minutes before the man came round. At least he couldn't be dead – that single blow had not been hard enough to kill him.

Had it?

Rollison felt the sharp edge of doubt. One man dead of a broken neck, one man unconscious from drugs, now this man lying in a crumpled heap, as if there were no life left in him.

Rollison lifted the girl bodily, and she was feather-light. He carried her to an easy-chair near the fireplace and dumped her into it while she still gasped for breath. He swung round towards the man on the floor, straightened him out, and tried his pulse.

It was beating.

Rollison felt as if he were choking.

He touched the back of the other's head. There was a bump and a small cut, and a little blood stained his fingers; nothing suggested serious injury. Rollison's own forehead was wet with the sweat of anxiety and of relief. He also felt momentarily dizzy. He stood quite still, not trying to fight against it, but allowing the spasm to die away. It lasted for a long time. He felt himself swaying, but still did not fight; and slowly his head cleared. He knew that if the man had come round in that moment he would not have had a chance, but the man lay very still, genuinely unconscious.

The girl's breathing was easier, but she lay back in the chair with her eyes closed and her mouth open. Rollison bent over the man and felt inside his pockets. There was a wallet, and he took it out and opened it; he found money, but nothing else at all. There were twenty pounds, all in old one-pound notes.

His other pockets were empty except for a handkerchief, a comb, and the kind of oddments a man usually carried. There were no tickets, no letters, nothing which could help to identify him. In short, he was as anonymous as the other two had been.

There was a kind of uncanniness about all this; about the situation altogether. Coincidence had a long arm, and Rollison would never reject it completely, but it was remarkable that this man should have been here at the very moment he, Rollison, had arrived. Why had he come? And why had he tried to choke the girl? To make sure that she could not talk?

Rollison stood up, cautiously. His head ached more than it had all that day; if it grew any worse, he would be practically useless. He looked down at the man, wondering how long the other would be unconscious; if he were shut in a cupboard, too, would he drug himself?

How could he, if his pockets were empty?

Rollison searched again, deeper into the partitions of the wallet, and found three small white tablets wrapped in cellophane. He had no doubt that these were tablets which could knock a man out and keep him out for hours. This was a refinement which not only puzzled but worried Rollison, for this man and those with him knew exactly what they wanted, and took precautions which would make the ordinary criminal look silly.

Who were they?

What were they trying to do?

Rollison crossed to the dressing-table, and took out several pairs of nylon stockings, used these as cords, and bound the man's wrists and ankles. At least he would be secure for the next hour, and longer, if necessary. The girl was still leaning back with her eyes closed and her mouth open; she no longer looked like the sex kitten. He went into the dining-room, where he had seen whisky and brandy, poured out a little brandy, and took it to her. He could picture little wizened Lil Ebbutt taking brandy obediently; and this girl, her eyes open now, opened her mouth obediently too, swallowed, and then tried to speak. Rollison told her to keep quiet for five minutes, and went into the drawing-room. He opened the bureau and ran through the papers there; mostly they were letters to Mrs. Cedric Dwight, and those written by friends all began in the same way: *Dear Kitty.* Kitty for kitten, Kitty for Kate. Kate was an impossible name for this girl. He made sure that there was nothing helpful, and then searched the sideboard in the diningroom, but drew another blank. He had a feeling of acute frustration: there would be nothing here, of course; this was a waste of time: except that he might be able to persuade his prisoner to talk.

The girl knew something, too.

He heard nothing when he went into the hall, and stepped into that fiery-looking spare bedroom. He was not normally susceptible to atmosphere, but this did not appeal to him at all. The fires seemed to burn and the smoke seemed to writhe, and each caricature of Mephistopheles seemed to take on life. What made a man design such a room?

Then Rollison made his discovery.

In one corner was a small bureau, and when he opened it he found it filled with sketches, patterns of wall-paper and of paints. It was remarkably tidy, and suggested someone who really knew what he was doing with colours. Rollison rifled through the sketches, and was not surprised to see some which had obviously been the basis for the work in this room. There were patterns of silks and satins, too; this desk belonged to an interior decorator, and whether he was amateur or professional did not greatly matter.

Each sketch was initialled: C.D.

Dwight?

Rollison found another book of sketches by the side of the bureau, and opened it with exceptional eagerness; this might at least throw some light on to Dwight. It did, quickly. There were sketches of women – many of the girl in the next room, many of the film stars round the walls. There were photographs, too; obviously this was Dwight's passion as well as his hobby. There was nothing remotely salacious or sexy about any of it; no Victorian boudoir would have been shamed to exhibit any of these pictures.

So Dwight was an artist, and a reasonably good one. He had probably designed this room.

And he suffered from delusions, or so it was said: the kind of thing which might influence a man's taste in such designs as these; which might twist and warp the fabric of his mind so that he could create a room of devils and of hell-fire. Was this evidence of a warped mind, or simply of a kind of thwarted genius?

There were no documents of any kind in here.

But there was a small diary, with some addresses in it, some telephone numbers, and, at the end of the diary pages, a column of different figures, like telephone numbers which had been doubled or trebled. It took only a moment for Rollison to know what this was: a list of the codes of a combination safe.

Was the safe here?

He stood up and looked round. There was only one small room he had not yet searched, and he went there at once – and found the safe under a picture. He felt a quickening excitement as he tried the combination he had found, and pulled the door open.

The safe was empty.

He felt a sharp anti-climax as he went back to the big room. A minute or two afterwards he heard the key turn in the lock.

Only the girl could have locked him in – only Cedric's wife. Rollison was quite sure that the man had been secure.

He went to the door almost as soon as the lock clicked home, and tried it with his shoulder. It was solid and firm and there was no hope of forcing it. His head throbbed even with that slight effort. He knelt down, taking a knife out of his pocket; it was a kind which Grice would have frowned upon but would make a burglar's heart glad. He could see nothing, for the key was in the lock. He thought he heard whispering. He kept trying to reconcile what had happened before with this: hadn't he *seen* the man try to strangle the girl?

Had she let him go free?

Or had she locked him, Rollison, in while she went for the police? Was this in fact an act of great courage?

Rollison pushed an awl against the key, felt it yield, and then heard it drop. He could see light, but there were no voices and no sounds. He opened the blade that served as a skeleton key and worked with it; he had never been in a greater hurry and it had never seemed to take so long. But at last he felt it get a grip; turned; and made the lock click back. The sound seemed so loud that anyone in the hall or near it must have heard. Cautiously, he opened the door. He could not be sure what would happen, and there was at least the possibility that he would be attacked.

Nothing happened.

Had the girl gone?

He stepped right into the hall. Every light in the flat seemed to be on, including those in the great drawing-room. He approached the doorway cautiously, but no one was in sight. He had one ear alert for any sound outside, trying to make up his mind what he would do if the police did arrive at her urgent call.

He heard the girl's footsteps, and swung round.

She was coming towards him from the bedroom. She had put on a housecoat which buttoned high at the neck; a Chinese dragon pattern in greens and golds. Somehow it made her look more mature. Her hair was absurdly silky and wavy. Her eyes still seemed huge. She watched him, as if wondering whether he would jump at her, but there was none of the fear which he had seen before; only wariness.

"Are you the Toff?" she asked, quite steadily.

"I used to be," answered Rollison, ruefully.

"I mean, are you Richard Rollison?"

"Yes."

"Did Cedric come to see you?"

"Yes."

"You mustn't help him," she said with sudden vehemence. "He'll be hurt if you do." She drew nearer, as if in defiance, and as if to make sure that he did not go past her into the room. "That man told me—"

"Why did you let him go?"

"Because he said that if I didn't, Cedric would be killed!" she answered hotly. "He told me that Cedric is a prisoner of some friends of his, and—well, I *had* to let him go. And he warned me that if you tried to help, then Cedric—"

She broke off.

She did not know it, but she was making one thing vividly clear to Rollison: that at all costs he was to be prevented from helping Cedric Dwight. Why was that so vital? What could he do that others couldn't? A great deal seemed to fall into place with this clear knowledge: the attack at the river, the attack on Ebbutt, anything to draw him away from Cedric Dwight himself.

Why?

And was this lovely little creature quite so innocent as she wanted to make out?

Chapter Thirteen

Pressures

"It's no use trying to make me change my mind or persuade me that he was bluffing," Kitty Dwight said. "He nearly strangled me—you saw him, didn't you? There's nothing he wouldn't do if I helped Cedric, or if I let you help him. Will you please leave this apartment?"

Rollison found it difficult not to smile. He wished that his head were not throbbing so much, wished even more that he could concentrate. The fact was that Kitty had allowed his one useful witness to go; everyone and everything seemed set on making it impossible to ask questions. There was the possibility that the man had choked her in order to frighten her; there was also the possibility that he had wanted to kill her, because of what she could say to him, the Toff. If that were so, there was still a chance of getting the information from her, but she would have to be frightened first.

He didn't relish that idea.

"If you won't go, I shall have to telephone the porter," Kitty announced, with that unbelievable earnestness. "Cedric once had to have a drunken man thrown out."

"Ah," said Rollison, gravely. "The porter must be a very strong man. Kitty, what makes you think you can save your husband by doing what a crook like that wants you to?"

"I know exactly what I'm doing," Kitty answered, and sounded as if she believed it. "Don't make any more trouble, it's been bad enough as it is." Her voice quivered, and Rollison knew that she was fighting desperately to put up this brave show. "Cedric said he would be back by half-past seven at the latest. I ordered dinner for eight o'clock, and let it get cold. I could hardly eat a mouthful as it was. And I'm so tired …"

She went on talking, complaining a little, and pleading. But she wasn't having the same effect on Rollison. Cedric had come to him, in terror and in hope; had agreed to stay the night at the flat; had appeared to be delighted and relieved at the prospect. He had not said that he was keeping anyone waiting, and surely he would have wanted to send a telephone message to his wife to say that he wouldn't be home.

He might have asked Jolly to do that, though; there may not have been time. True, Jolly hadn't said anything about it.

"… and if you don't go, I really will call the porter," Kitty was saying, and the pleading note in her voice was much more noticeable. "I don't *want* trouble, but—"

"Kitty," Rollison said, and stepped towards her, "why did you let that man go?"

"I've told you! He said he would kill Cedric!"

"Why did you let him go?"

"*I've told you!*" she gasped, and backed away, her hand outstretched towards the telephone near the bed. She could have screamed, but did not. She could have lifted the telephone, but did not. "Go away from me!"

"Don't call the porter," Rollison warned. "Call the police. They're much better chuckers out than porters." He went still nearer, but she did not touch the telephone, just seemed to want to shrink away from him. "Why did you let that man out? What can he do to Cedric?"

She cried: "He can kill him!"

"He can do something else. What is it? What's really frightening your husband?" Rollison held her wrists in his hands, wrists which were thin and cool and tiny. The girl was very close to him, trying to pull herself free, but unable to. His voice was rougher as he went on: "Why should men pretend to kill him? What are they trying to make him do?"

"I don't know!" Kitty cried. "I only know that man said they would kill Cedric if I didn't let him go. And Cedric's absolutely terrified. You've seen him, you must know he is. He can't walk outside without looking over his shoulder, he isn't safe wherever he goes. That's why he came to see you, but—"

"I can help him."

"You can't. No one can. He's a prisoner, isn't he?" When Rollison didn't answer, Kitty went on fiercely: "Is he or isn't he? Didn't he come to you and stay in your flat for safety—and didn't you let these men take him away? How much help do you think you are?"

She couldn't be blamed for thinking like that; a lot of people would think with her, and among them was Rollison himself. He wasn't sure whether to believe her; he simply knew that he could not handle a slip of a girl like this effectively.

"How long have you been married?" he demanded abruptly.

"Three months on Friday, but what's that to do with it?" It practically convinced Rollison that she was Dwight's wife, but he didn't say so. "Why don't you go away you—you imitation detective! You aren't helping Cedric, you're only doing him harm."

Rollison let her go, chuckling at the vehemence in her voice and the glitter in her eyes. The chuckle became a laugh which he could not keep back. He knew that he was nearly hysterical from fatigue, shock, call it what he liked. He wanted to go on laughing, and he scared her. In a way he scared himself.

Then he realised that he must not leave her here alone, that she might be able to tell him much more than she had said. There was one way to get her away without difficulty. He had those three tablets in his pocket—

Were they simply morphine? He couldn't be sure. But he could be sure that Jolly had some tablets which would act like knock-out drops; it was only a question of getting them here.

Then Kitty yawned.

One moment she had been so scared that her eyes had looked enormous, as if she would never close them willingly; and then she gave a great yawn, so that he could see her pink and shiny tongue, and the perfect rows of teeth. In yawning, her eyes closed. She clapped her hand to her mouth and looked scared; then she yawned again, even more widely.

"Get out of here!" she cried, as if fear suddenly took complete possession of her. "Get out, get out!"

She flung herself at him and began to beat his chest with her clenched fist, and she had more strength than her small body promised. Rollison let her vent her fury, saw her caught out with a yawn in the middle of it, and realised that she could not keep herself awake.

Had she drugged herself knowingly?

Rollison moved swiftly, holding her so close that she could not strike or move, and the warmth of her lovely young body touched him. She strained her head back and kept crying at him, but he continued to smile at her, holding her very tight, until suddenly her eyes closed. She opened them again quickly, fought to keep them open, but there was much less strength in her blows, less vigour in her voice, and her eyes looked so heavy that she could not hope to keep awake.

"Give it up, Kitty," Rollison urged.

He changed his hold on her as she relaxed – just held her against his right arm, with her head against his chest. If anyone came in, this would tell its own false story. Kitty looked up at him, stifled a yawn, and said falteringly: "Don't let them hurt Cedric. Don't let them, please."

"I won't," he promised. "Just relax, and take it easy."

She let her head droop, and in a few minutes he knew that she was in a deep sleep. He lifted her to a chair, sat her in it, and then raised the lid of her left eye. She had been drugged with one of the morphines, exactly like the man at Gresham Terrace, almost certainly with pills like those he had taken from the wallet of the man who had escaped from here.

The most urgent question was whether she had drugged herself so that she could not be compelled to talk. Could fear for her husband drive her as far as that?

Rollison was looking at her when the telephone bell rang, startling in the silence. That would be Wrightson. He looked at his watch; it was exactly the half-hour. Thinking of Wrightson forced him to think of Bill Ebbutt, and to wonder how Bill was. So much happened that he had no time to think clearly or to plan; he was being forced to take swift evasive or aggressive action whether he wanted to or not, and it seemed certain that someone meant to make sure that he could not really concentrate.

He lifted the telephone.

"Hallo," he said, cautiously.

"If you're not out of that flat in five minutes, we're coming to get you," a man said. "Don't expect any help from your bruiser pal, either. He's having a sleep."

That should not have taken Rollison by surprise; but it did.

He put down the receiver slowly, and felt himself colder than he had been for a long time, touched with the fear which came so often in this case. They almost certainly meant what they said. There was little they could not do, little they did not guess. They had followed Wrightson, of course; or else they had watched this great building. It did not matter which way they had come; they had pushed him out on a limb again.

Of course, he could call the police.

Being here would take a lot of explaining away. The Honourable Richard Rollison, alone in an apartment with a young married woman who was unconscious. He could picture the headlines if the Press got hold of it; he could picture the faces of the Divisional men, for that matter. But what the Press, the police or the public thought was supremely unimportant. The essential thing was to preserve his own freedom of action. It would be extremely difficult to talk his way out of some kind of charge, even if Grice were on his side. There were rules which the police had to obey and the Toff could ignore, but ignoring them created its own problems. By sending for the police he could make quite sure no harm came to him now, but he would almost certainly be prevented from working on the job all next day; perhaps even for longer. And he had three jobs to do. There was another reason why he must not telephone the police. If he turned to them for help, he would weaken his own hand to danger point. He was the Toff, the lone wolf, the man who drove through regardless of danger. The prestige and the impact of the Toff would be halved if it were known that he had called the Yard for help now. It had to appear to be the other way round: the Toff helping the Yard. Moreover, the Yard believed Bob Benning guilty; the Yard had failed to find the motor-cyclist mob. If he could prove Benning innocent, and could smash the motor-cyclists, his stock would rise enormously – and Bill Ebbutt's East End would do whatever he wanted. While Ebbutt was out of action, that was a vital thing.

The man who had telephoned him almost certainly knew that.

He had been given five minutes, and two of them were gone already.

He began to smile, for he had decided what to do.

He crossed to the drawing-room, where the lights were still on, went to the window, and saw the small balcony outside. He also saw the railing of the balcony at the window next door, and although it would be a long drop if he fell, there was no need to fall. He looked down into the lamplit street and into the darkness of Hyde Park. A solitary policeman was strolling along the street, and a car passed. No one stood about, no one appeared to be watching; and there was no reason why they should watch, because the entrances were in the side streets, not in Park Lane.

Three minutes had gone.

Would "they" be punctual?

He opened the French windows, and then went back to the bedroom. It was a warm night, and the girl would come to no harm in that housecoat and those drainpipe trousers. He lifted her, and her head lolled against his shoulder. He was smiling faintly as he carried her to the French windows and edged outside, careful not to bang her head against the wooden framework; but her feet caught it on the other side.

He saw no one below.

It was easy to hoist the girl over on to the next balcony, and for a moment he thought that he would join her, force the French windows of the next apartment, and so take her away. But some men might still be watching the entrances; not all of the men were likely to come up here. He eased Kitty down until she was sitting with her back against the wall of the next-door room, then hurried back to the bedroom, picked up the satin-covered eiderdown, and took it to her. He watched the deserted street as he placed it over her; only her feet showed. He did not vault over, to cover her completely, for six or seven minutes had now passed, and he did not think that the man on the telephone would be very late.

He shut the French windows immediately, and went into the hall, and immediately heard a sound at the door.

He also heard a sound from the kitchen; so men were trying to get in at both back and front.

They were quite as good as their word.

Chapter Fourteen

Checkmate?

Rollison heard both sounds quite clearly, and felt sure that one door or the other would be forced before long. Even bolted and chained, he could have opened either of them if given time. He tapped his pockets, first for the gas pistol with its pellets of knock-out gas, next for the automatic. Then he went into the dining-room and poured himself a stiff whisky; he needed it badly, head and hangover or not. Now he was beginning to feel worried about Wrightson, and also about the fact that it took him so long to decide what to do.

He went into the bedroom and dialled his flat. The men outside could not hear him talking from there.

The ringing sound started at once, and then seemed to go on and on for so long that he began to feel worried, in case there had been more trouble at Gresham Terrace. Then there was a break in the ringing sound, and Jolly announced: "This is the Honourable Richard Rollison's residence," as crisply and formally as if this were the middle of the morning, not the midnight hours.

"Hallo, Jolly," Rollison said. "How are things?"

"There is no change here, sir," Jolly answered promptly. "I telephoned the hospital at half-past twelve, and was told that there was no change in Mr. Ebbutt's condition either."

"That could be worse, then. Jolly, I don't know how they did it, but some of the opposition party has put Wrightson to sleep. He was in an alley between Midd Street and the Apex building, and I think someone ought to go and see if he's still there, and lend him a hand. Use the Morris and ask Wrightson's buddy to fix added protection, will you?"

"At once, sir. And you—"

"Don't worry about me," said Rollison reassuringly, and there was laughter in his voice; the whisky was already having its effect. "I'm doing fine with a sleeping beauty, none other than Cedric Dwight's wife. Did he tell you about her?"

"Well no, sir," answered Jolly, "but he did ask if he could telephone a message, and I allowed him to. He left a message for a lady who appeared to be named Kitty."

"That's the girl," said Rollison. "Listen very carefully. She is having a nap on the balcony of Apartment 226. If I'm not back by six o'clock make some arrangements to get her away. If it really becomes necessary, tell the police where she is, but avoid them at this stage if you can."

"I will see to it, sir," promised Jolly, as if he had been asked to take a suit to the cleaners; then he went on with obvious anxiety: "Are you sure you will be all right?"

"Positive," said Rollison. "I'll be seeing you."

He rang off.

The odd thing was that he meant exactly what he said: he believed that he would have no serious trouble. He took out cigarettes and lit one, and then went into the hall. He heard a faint noise, and saw that the top bolt was being eased back by a strip of very fine high-tensile steel; a beautifully expert job of forcing entry. The bottom bolt was still in position, but the lock had been forced. He went into the kitchen, where men outside were obviously still working on the door and the lock. He pulled the refrigerator from the point and heaved and pushed until it was across the door to the fire escape, then placed a chair and a table into a position so that no one could get in that way. Then he began to whistle, quite loudly. He went to the front door, shot the top bolt so quickly that he made the man with the tool cry out, and unfastened the bottom bolt. He opened the door and stood aside, looking into the faces of two men who stood so astounded that they had made no move either to attack or run away.

"Why, hallo," greeted Rollison, amiably. "Forget your key?" He stood aside and gestured to them. "Come in, do, but don't come too close, or I might get angry."

One of these was the man whom Kitty had allowed to escape; the other was a stranger. They had much in common, for they were men of medium height, wiry, strong-looking; not big, but obviously tough. One of them dropped his hand to his pocket and brought out a gun.

"Don't make a noise," urged Rollison. "I believe there's a baby next door."

"You stay where you are," the man ordered sharply.

"Do we have to shout?" protested the Toff, and beamed at them.

They were puzzled because they had not the faintest idea why he was so sure of himself; they would probably never understand. He drew at his cigarette, keeping his hands in sight, and took no notice at all of the other's automatic. Both men had recovered from the initial surprise, and one of them moved swiftly into the bedroom, while the other covered Rollison as if ready to shoot at the slightest move.

The man came out of the bedroom.

"Where is she?" he demanded.

"Sleeping Beauty?" asked Rollison, blandly. "She didn't like it here any longer, so I let her go away."

"Don't talk out of the back of your neck. She's in this flat."

"Two magicians in conflict, that should be interesting," said Rollison, and seemed really delighted. "I waved a wand and said abracadabra, and presumably you're going to wave yours and say the word backwards. May I listen and watch?"

"You talk too much. Where is she?"

"My dear chap! Don't you know?"

"Go and look for her," the man with the gun ordered his companion. "She's about somewhere."

"If you find her, give her my love," said Rollison, and moved to a table and leaned against it.

The man with the gun was watching him closely, and was palpably suspicious of a trick. Neither of them spoke, while the second of the intruders stormed from room to room. Obviously he looked under beds and inside wardrobes and cupboards; as obviously he opened every door, slamming some of them, and muttering to himself. It was five minutes before he came back to the hall, and there was an ugly expression on a hard, thin face.

"I can't find her."

The man with the gun demanded savagely: "Where is she, Rollison?"

"You must take your choice," said Rollison, brightly. "I'm told there are five hundred apartments in the building, and she's in one of them. I have friends—didn't you know? You gave me just time to get her out and come back to say hallo. You want her, I've got her. You've got Cedric, and I want him. We could do a deal, couldn't we?"

"If you don't tell us where she is, I'll put a bullet into you," said the man with the gun flatly.

Rollison crossed his ankles and shifted his position so that he was much more comfortable. Outwardly he seemed nonchalant, but in fact he was not feeling nonchalant at all. The man might mean what he said. Here was the moment of crisis; the moment for the other to call his bluff. One shot could do terrible harm, and there was nothing at all he could do to prevent the man from shooting.

Would he want the Toff injured?

Would he believe that an injured man would talk more freely?

Rollison did not shift his position again. The seconds ticked by. His forehead felt warm, and he knew that there was a beading of sweat on it, but he did not touch it with his hand, and he maintained his smile. He heard the heavy breathing of each man; they wanted to shoot, but they were not sure that it would help them. So as he had hoped, above everything else they wanted Kitty Dwight.

A minute must have passed.

"Make up your mind, I'm getting quite stiff," murmured Rollison.

He straightened up from the table – and then without the slightest warning leapt at the man with the gun. He glimpsed the startled look, and the tensing of muscles, knew that the shot was coming, and flopped down. The bullet zipped over his head. He clutched the man's legs round the knees, heaved, and brought him crashing; there was another shot, a soft sneeze of sound, a thud, and a little shower of plaster. He reached the other side of the hall, his own automatic in his right hand, while the other man's gun was on the floor.

"How does it feel to be on the receiving end?" he inquired. "If you're anxious to learn the trick, it is largely psychological. You bluff the other chap into thinking that you've been turned into a pillar of stone, and at the crucial moment you prove that you haven't. Of course you might get a bullet where it hurts—it depends on whether the risk is worthwhile. Turn round. And you on the floor—get up, and face the wall."

The standing man hesitated, and then turned. Rollison moved to him, tapped his coat and arms and legs, made sure that he was not carrying a gun, and backed away. Then he picked up the other man's gun, as its owner got slowly to his feet and turned to face the wall. Rollison opened the gun and looked inside; it was fully loaded. Now that the immediate crisis was over, he felt hot, as well as uneasy in his stomach; he needed another drink.

"Supposing we try to make sense out of this," he suggested, with an effort. "What has Cedric Dwight got that you want?"

Neither man answered.

"What makes you try to frighten the life out of him?" asked Rollison. "Will it help if you drive him off his head?

There couldn't be anything in that, could there? I mean, who would benefit if Cedric was proved to be *non compos mentis*? Uncle, brothers, cousins, or aunts? I haven't much time to inquire into the family tree of the hapless Cedric, but it shouldn't take long. It could take even less time if you start talking. My—ah—name is Rollison. People call me the Toff, and I have quite a reputation. You could ask some of Ebbutt's friends, and they'll tell you that if I think the cause is just, I will gladly break a man's neck or other parts of his anatomy. This is a hard world," he went on with great earnestness, "and when dealing with animals one occasionally has to behave like an animal, no matter how repugnant it is. I feel, in fact," he said more softly, and flicked the safety catch of his own automatic so that they could hear the sound. "I feel the urge to be animalistic now. Ebbutt was a close friend of mine. You showed him no mercy. You didn't show any mercy to me when you threw me in the river, either."

A man turned his head. He was sweating and he was grey, and his mouth was working.

"We don't know anything," he exclaimed. "We only do what we're told. That's God's truth."

Rollison moved, and rapped the man's head with his knuckles, made him stagger forward towards the wall. He felt as furious and bitter as he sounded, not for himself, nor even for Cedric Dwight and his terror, but because of what had happened to Bill Ebbutt.

"Who are you working for? I'll give you thirty seconds to answer."

Then, he heard footsteps on the carpeted passage outside; running footsteps. Both of the prisoners turned their heads towards the door, as if in hope. Rollison backed a pace so that he could cover them and the newcomer. He saw the third, small man, who pulled up short at sight of the gun, whose mouth was open, and who gasped: "The police are coming! There are two cars, waiting at the corner."

There was nothing to be done about it, Rollison admitted gloomily. Ten more minutes, even five more, and he might have wrung some useful information out of these men; now, he had to let them go, or make sure that they would tell the police all they could about him.

Did that matter?

He did not know how it was that the police had come, or what had caused an alarm. There was an outside chance that it was to do with trouble in another part of Apex House, but that was hardly likely. A car at each corner meant that they were planning to converge; and also meant to make sure that no wanted man could escape from here.

More thoughts flashed through Rollison's mind.

If these men were held by the police, there would be three less to work against, and that could do no harm.

One man swung round: "You've no more right here than we have. If the cops—"

"But they know I'm here to look after Cedric and his Kitty," said Rollison brightly.

He slipped the gas pistol from his pocket, and pulled the trigger so that the gas billowed about the faces of the two men by the wall. The messenger turned and ran, and Rollison did not attempt to stop him, just saw the horror in the faces of the two men who had seen him pull the trigger and who doubtless thought of death.

They began to choke as the gas bit at their nostrils and their throats.

He pushed them backwards, into the main bedroom, slammed the door and locked it on them, and then hurried to the front door. He heard the thud of footsteps, but nothing else. He was hot and sticky, and his head was throbbing, but his spirits were higher than they had been since Isobel had come to see him. Isobel. Was she sleeping the sleep of the innocent, or was she sleepless because of the danger to her boy? Was there also danger to her? Should she be watched?

He heard footsteps, not far away, and knew that the police were hurrying. It would be useless to run, and pointless to try to get away. The only thing worth trying was to persuade them that the raiders had spirited Kitty Dwight away.

Chapter Fifteen

Morning

Three men appeared in the entrance of the flat, all large and massive, and only one of them familiar to Rollison; but that one was a godsend. His name was Bryant, he was now a Chief Inspector, and at one time had been a detective sergeant in serious trouble; the kind of trouble which might have condemned him to the ranks for a long time to come. Rollison had seen the trap into which he had fallen, opened it, and enabled him to escape.

In a dozen ways since Bryant had shown real gratitude. He was obviously in charge of the trio, for he was a middle-aged man, and the others were in their early thirties. He pulled up short at the sight of the Toff, then he gave a curiously one-sided grin.

"They told me you were mixed up in this business, but I didn't think you'd let us take you red-handed," he said. "What's the excuse this time?"

"At least I've got no alibi," said Rollison, almost sadly. "I'm just a much-misunderstood man."

"See who else is about," said Bryant to the two detectives. Looking curiously at Rollison as if at an exhibit in a zoo, they obeyed. They would soon find the two unconscious men, but neither victim would be able to talk for at least half an hour. "Well, Mr. Rollison. Have you any right to be there?"

"The right of a loyal citizen," said Rollison, earnestly, and then surprised the other by adding: "Mind if I sit down? I've had about all I can take."

"Something to hear you admit it," said Bryant. "What with the river episode and the trouble at Whitechapel, you ought to have been in bed hours ago." He waited until Rollison sat in an easy-chair by the side of a table with a few glossy magazines on it, as if in a doctor's waiting-room. He was not only big and broad, but very thick-set, he had a square chin and a rather flattened face, almost too broad; his short nose and short upper-lip did not make him look handsome; just strong. "What are you doing here?"

"I came to see if Dwight was home."

"There's a message from Mr. Grice saying that he's at your place."

"The mills of the Yard grind slowly, but they grind exceedingly fine," said Rollison, heavily. He took out cigarettes, but Bryant shook his head, and Rollison lit one. "He was at the flat, but was spirited away. Jolly was shanghaied. I caught one of the gentry responsible, but he took a sleeping pill, and so he can't be persuaded to talk. I'd promised Dwight I'd help in every way I could, and he was nervous about his wife, who was here alone, so I came to see if I could help her."

He looked and sounded grim as he said that.

"Could you?" inquired Bryant.

"Arrived too late," declared Rollison.

Bryant looked at him from narrowed eyes, as if trying to assess the situation thoroughly, not convinced that he was hearing the truth.

"There were two chaps here, and I ran straight into them," Rollison went on. "We had a bit of a shindy, and I managed to put them to sleep." He paused; and almost immediately heard an exclamation from one of the other men. "Your chaps seem to have found 'em," he added dryly. "I was trying to make them come across when a scout they'd stationed outside said that you were on the way. What brought you?"

"We had a telephone call from the night porter, who said that some men had broken in and were on the fifth floor," Bryant answered. "We found two motor-cycles parked nearby—and each one had double registration plates, so we knew what to expect. Did these fellows talk?"

"They said they acted under orders, but wouldn't say from whom."

"Hmm."

"Hmm, what?"

"Pity we came so soon," said Bryant, dryly. "They might talk to us, but they'd much more likely to talk to you. Is Mrs. Dwight here?"

"No."

"Do you know where she is?"

"I wish I did," said Rollison, without batting an eye. "I think she would probably talk to me with a little persuasion, but I doubt if she would to the police. She seemed to think that her dear Cedric was in some kind of trouble, and that it wouldn't do for the police to know about it. Of course, I might be wrong," Rollison added, as airily as he could, "but I'd like to think I could have half an hour's talk with her first."

Bryant's deep-set eyes were crinkling at the corners. He knew exactly what the Toff meant, and was going to accept the situation. A different type of man, or one who did not owe the Toff a debt, would try to force the issue, would hector him and be obtuse.

Suddenly, Rollison yawned.

Bryant said: "I've seen men tired, but never more tired than you look, Mr. Rollison. Will you sign a statement in the morning?"

"Glad to."

"Is your car here?"

"Don't say your chaps didn't recognise my T-model Ford!"

Bryant chuckled. "I thought you drove a Rolls-Bentley; didn't know that you'd come down in the world. You'd be better off if—"

He stopped, looking at his two men who appeared from the bedroom, to report their find. They had tried to bring the three men round, but had no effect at all. As they finished, there were more footsteps outside, and to his great relief, Rollison saw Wrightson come in. There was an ugly bruise over Percy's right eye, and a cut on one side of his mouth, but his eyes were bright and alert.

"Never wanted to see a man more," declared Rollison. "Chief Inspector Bryant was going to offer to run me home, and you know what it's like riding in a police car. Or don't you?" Wrightson gave a quick grin, and Bryant kept a straight face; the two men were very much alike in some ways, but Bryant was the more massive. "Is Jolly outside?"

"No, sir. He returned to the flat," answered Wrightson.

"I hope he's turning my bed down," said Rollison. "This is a night when I want someone to undress me. All clear, Chief Inspector?"

"Until the morning."

"Thanks," said Rollison, warmly.

He went out with Wrightson, watched by curious policemen on duty in the passage and at the lift. He passed the door of Number 226, and wondered whether there was any chance that the police would find Kitty: they had only to step right out on to the balcony. There was nothing he could do about it, and just then nothing that he wanted to do. He had a fit of yawning, which reminded him of Kitty, and kept on yawning on the way to the old Ford. He bent down and got in as Wrightson opened the door – and bumped his head, because he saw Kitty Dwight in the back of the car, still dead to the world.

"Jolly and me fixed it," Wrightson said, with deep satisfaction. "Got her out just in time." He grinned crookedly. "That man Jolly's a proper caution. Never seen a man of his age move so quickly, and the way he picked the lock of the flat next door to Dwight's place—strike a light, it would give the cops the belly-ache for a fortnight. There's a garage right underneath. Jolly took us through that way, and parked the old Ford just inside so the cops wouldn't take any notice of it. Then he went off in the Morris. I tell you, he's a proper caution." Wrightson took the wheel as if he were used to the car, and glanced over his shoulder. "She's a bit of all right, too, if you ask me. Don't come much prettier. Where'd you think she got that outfit?"

"Limehouse, Chinatown," Rollison said, solemnly.

Wrightson actually guffawed.

By the time they were at Gresham Terrace, however, he was his more solemn if not saturnine self. Rollison opened the front door, and Wrightson lifted the girl out and carried her upstairs. No one appeared to be watching, and certainly no one followed on their heels. Jolly was at the open front door of the flat, and except that his eyes had a glassy look, of tiredness, he seemed his usual self.

"I'm very glad to see you back, sir."

"I'm even glad to be back," Rollison said. "I hear you've been qualifying for the Houdini stakes."

"It was really a matter of timing, sir," Jolly answered. "I left immediately I could, and luckily found Mr. Wrightson staggering to the Ford. He soon recovered. I doubt very much whether it would have been possible to bring the young lady away but for Mr. Wrightson."

Jolly's tone was positively warm as he looked towards the boxer.

"Teamwork and timing, that's what it was," declared Wrightson. "I've dumped the dame on the spare bed. That okay?"

"I'll see to her," said Jolly. "Have you any idea how long she is likely to sleep, sir?"

"If she took what I think she took, eight or nine hours," said Rollison. "How about the Sleeping Beast?"

"He is still unconscious, sir," Jolly answered, and made his way to the spare room.

Wrightson watched him with an expression of unwilling admiration, and then gave his one-sided grin.

"I tell you," he announced earnestly, "he's a proper caution. Now, Mr. Ar, it's time you put your head down; you want twelve hours straight. Don't worry about anything else, Jolly and me will see to it. Anyone who can get away with what you've got away with to-night couldn't never go wrong. There's just one thing," he added, looking at Rollison with his head on one side, and the light of interest in his steady grey eyes.

"What's that?" inquired Rollison.

"Any idea what all this is about?"

"Not a notion," said Rollison, sadly, "and there's only one consolation. There hasn't been much time to find out."

He went into his bedroom.

Jolly had laid out his pyjamas and dressing-gown and turned down the bed. Sight of it made him feel so tired that the thought of brushing his teeth was revolting. But he brushed them, and shed his clothes, draping them carelessly over a chair. When he got into bed a clock in the next room struck four. It was not much more than twelve hours since he had talked to the Benning mission.

Bob Benning, Isobel Cole, Mrs. Benning. What were they feeling and what had he done to help them? Talked to Grice, had a word with Ebbutt, asked Ebbutt's men to make inquiries, put the Salvation Army on the trail! Well, that wasn't unreasonable in a few hours; there was no reason why he should reproach himself. The speed of events was the cause of the trouble, and he knew from experience that when a case began with such speed it seldom slackened.

This Dwight affair might finish to-morrow, and by that time the first odds and ends of information about Bob Benning and Marjorie Fryer should come in. He might be able to take that inquiry up with a completely free mind, after all. It would still be a double case.

He found himself smiling vaguely.

He felt himself going off into a heavy sleep, and knew that if a ton weight fell on him he would hardly be aware of it. Nothing mattered but sleep.

And Ebbutt; Ebbutt, who might be dying.

Bob Benning, and his sweetheart and his mother.

Cedric Dwight.

Kitty.

Little Kitty Dwight, fighting him and yawning at the same time – and now in the next bedroom, quite safe. Well, as safe as she could be anywhere. Of course she was safe. Safe as houses. He would talk to her in the morning.

He heard faint sounds when he woke, and saw that the sun was fairly high, for it was shining on to a patch of carpet near the window. Although he noticed this it was some time before he realised its significance: that it must be eleven o'clock. It was a very bright patch of sunlight, and he was too warm in bed. He wriggled his toes. He felt stiff and his head was tender, as if the skin were being stretched across his scalp. Ah! He did not jerk up, but was wide awake on the instant, and began to collect his thoughts. First, how was Ebbutt? Then, were there any developments?

He pushed back the bedclothes.

The silence inside the flat was complete, and for the first time he began to wonder whether anything was wrong. Things could happen without the slightest warning, and there was no way of being sure that the night had been trouble free. He swayed as he stood up, pressed the heels of his thumbs against his eyes, steadied, and crossed to the door. As he reached it, he heard footsteps, and Jolly said: "Yes, madam."

All was well!

Rollison went back to his bed and was sitting on it when Jolly came in, clad in his uniform of black coat, striped trousers, and cravat with its neat diamond tie-pin. He looked spruce, partly because he had had a haircut the previous morning, before any of this had begun, and partly because there was a kind of eternal youthfulness in him.

He would not be looking like this if there were bad news.

"Good morning, sir," said Jolly.

"'Morning. Ebbutt?"

"He passed a fair night, sir, and I understand from the hospital authorities that every hour that he survives, the better his chances."

"Ah."

"As I did not wish to make a nuisance of myself on the telephone, I have arranged with the secretary to telephone a report every four hours," said Jolly. "I think that she was persuaded to do so by the stories in the morning newspapers." He produced the newspaper like a conjurer producing rabbits from a hat, and held them out. "I will get your tea, sir."

"Yes. Where's Percy Wrightson?"

"Washing up, sir."

Rollison grinned. "He doesn't know how much of a caution you are! Thanks, Jolly. What about our other guests?"

"Mrs. Dwight is awake, and I have endeavoured to persuade her that it is in her interests to stay here and to co-operate," said Jolly. "She is anxious to return home, as she appears to think that if she does not, her husband is likely to suffer a great deal. On the other hand, she is obviously anxious not to be questioned by the police, and on balance I think that we shall find her co-operative."

"Good. And the man?"

"He is also awake, sir. Mr. Wrightson and I found it advisable to secure him, and he is now in my bedroom, sitting in a chair and tied to it by the arms and the legs. He is not very co-operative, and simply insists that he knows nothing that would be of the slightest use to us. I am inclined to think that he is right."

"Jolly," Rollison said, softly.

"Sir?"

"That's your first boob on this case."

"I am sorry to hear that, sir," Jolly said, looking surprised and even perturbed. "Would you be good enough to explain?"

"Yes. If this man thought it worthwhile taking a drug to make sure that he couldn't be questioned, he must know some of the answers, mustn't he?"

Jolly raised his hands, as if astounded, and then said in tones of great humility: "How very remiss of me, sir, not to think of that. You are quite right, of course. But may I suggest that you postpone the interrogation until after breakfast?"

Chapter Sixteen

Interrogation

Rollison ate a substantial breakfast …

He felt much more himself, and except for tenderness at his head, no serious ill effects from any of the events of the previous day. His problem was to consider those events in the right order, and to give each its proper emphasis. It was still difficult to judge which had been of greatest significance, and he kept reminding himself with an earnestness worthy of Jolly that it would be a mistake to try to reach conclusions too quickly. One mistake might be his last.

Dwight was still missing.

Rollison had no great regard of Cedric, but any human being who was victim of such fears was a man to help.

The newspapers gave large headlines and vivid pictures on the Battle of the East End Gym. Ebbutt's face, with his broken nose and his huge double chin, stared up from most of the front pages; and he was described as the "famous East London trainer". Probably he had never been so described before. There were pictures of the wreckage and, of course, there was also one of the Toff.

There was no mention of Dwight, but there was a passing reference to the incident on the Embankment even in the more exclusive papers, and a photograph of the Toff, dripping wet, in five of the popular dailies. Alongside this picture was another taken when he had been at a society wedding only a few months ago. He grinned at that alertness of the editorial mind, made sure that there was nothing in any of the newspapers which really helped, then pondered deeply on the attitude of the police.

Bryant had been almost too helpful.

Last night that had seemed a matter for congratulation, and simply his good luck at being interrogated by a man who was in his debt. But Bryant was also a policeman, and a good one. He could have helped without, in effect, allowing the Toff to do exactly what he wanted. There should have been a more stringent questioning.

Now that he thought back it was almost as if Bryant had wanted him to get away. Could that be so?

It was now nearly midday, and there was no word from the police. He could not be sure why not, but the beginning of an idea was already in his mind.

Did they want him to act on his own?

Were they more keenly aware of the circumstances and the issue at stake? Did they know that there were obstacles to them making quick progress and believe that he had a chance of finding the answers before they did? Such situations were rare, but there had been others. Grice himself had never hesitated to allow the Toff a free hand if he thought it would be to the Yard's advantage.

Grice had been emphatic that Dwight was a case of deluded mentality. Was that in fact what he believed? He was a cunning man as well as a first-class detective, and would know that if he scoffed at the idea that Dwight was in trouble, it would be likely to make the Toff delve very deeply.

Many puzzling things would be easily explained if the police were deliberately giving him rope.

Ah!

As Wrightson put it, Jolly was a proper caution, but there had been very little time for Jolly to work in while at Apex House. If the police had deliberately turned a blind eye, however, then the success of Jolly's swift move was easier to understand. So was the fact that the Gresham Terrace flat, was now, apparently, being watched. That had also puzzled Rollison last night, but he had been so tired that he had not given it much thought.

"Bill Grice," Rollison said to himself, "I would very much like a word with you."

He stood up from the breakfast table, with its litter of newspapers, and went into the kitchen. There he saw an almost unbelievable thing. Jolly was preparing a plump chicken for the oven, and Wrightson was peeling potatoes.

"My lucky day," the ex-boxer said promptly. "When I'm at 'ome, the old woman expects me to do the spuds for the family. I wouldn't care if it was only me own kids, but what wiv' my bruvvers and 'er sisters—"

Rollison said: "You can come and work here whenever you like. I promise you that Jolly will acquire no brothers or sisters."

He went out, and paused outside the door of the spare bedroom. He heard radio music. He was tempted to look in, but did not, just checked that the door was locked on the outside. Jolly was taking no chances. The spare-room window was of toughened glass, and there was electrical control to the catch; no doubt that would be fastened securely, too. Rollison passed along a small passage, and opened the door of Jolly's small bedroom.

It was a remarkable room, for against a wall there was a workbench filled with pigeon-holes, all of which were filled with some tool or *aide* to the craft of detection. It was like a tiny but well-equipped police laboratory, a kind of miniature police station. For years Jolly had worked to build this, but only recently had he gone to such trouble as he did these days. He could take fingerprints, and develop photographs, make keys, force locks – do nearly everything that a detective would want to do when he was away from the scene of the crime, checking his clues.

Sitting in an old-fashioned armchair, and securely fastened to it, was the man whom Rollison had caught last night. He was smaller than Rollison had remembered, tough-looking like all of the men involved; and that made Rollison pause. These men were in excellent training, a fact which it would be easy to forget. Whatever job they usually did demanded extreme physical fitness; and he would not be surprised to know that they all trained to keep in condition.

Boxers? Runners? Footballers? Cricketers?

It was guesswork.

He knew that there was nothing in the man's pockets that would help, and he saw the defiance in the clear grey eyes. This man could be a very useful customer in a tight corner. He had been unconscious for a long time, and badly shaken before that, but there was a calmness in his manner which told Rollison that he was very sure of himself. He looked quite unafraid.

Yet he had drugged himself rather than allow himself to be questioned the previous night.

Why, if he were not afraid that he could be made to talk?

Rollison stood by the door, looking at him, and the man returned his gaze with that unexpectedly fearless expression; he was not really brazen, just bold. He had close-cut, black hair, he needed a shave, and his lips were set tightly. The longer Rollison looked at him, the tougher he looked. He did not speak, and seemed determined on this silent defiance.

Rollison said: "Where is Cedric Dwight?"

The man did not answer.

"You know," Rollison said. "Where is he?"

Still the man did not answer.

"Who employs you?" Rollison demanded, but he realised that he could ask questions by the dozen and get no response at all, unless he could find a way of unnerving this man. The period of unconsciousness had apparently strengthened his nerve; that might have been one of the reasons why he had taken the tablets.

"Three of your friends were arrested last night," Rollison announced.

The man stared back, impassively.

There might be some point in trying to frighten him physically, but Rollison did not think that would succeed, and he did not relish the task himself. This situation needed cunning, not force; and it was at least conceivable that he did not know anything worth passing on.

Rollison called: "Jolly!"

Jolly came quickly, dusting his hands.

"Has this man had anything to eat or drink?"

"A cup of tea, sir."

"Give him something to eat," Rollison ordered.

"Very good, sir."

"I'll see him again early this afternoon," said Rollison. "Tie him up again after he's eaten. All clear?"

"Perfectly clear, sir," Jolly said.

"Good. As soon as he's fed, bring in all the electric fires we have, and plug them into this room—you're full of points," Rollison pointed out. "Shut the window and shut the door. Get it really hot, like a Turkish bath. All understood?"

"Perfectly," Jolly said.

The man's eyes shifted for the first time, to the one electric fire near him, to Rollison, and then to the window. It was already stuffy in here, and the bright sunlight outside told of the warmth of the day.

"Let's see if we can sweat some sense into him," Rollison went on. "And then tell Wrightson to send for the masseur at the gymnasium. We'll give the fellow a good work out, and hope his memory has improved by then."

Rollison nodded curtly, and went out. He saw the expression in the prisoner's face. Was this the beginning of a breakdown? Rollison went to the spare-room door, hesitated again, then turned the key in the lock, and tapped. The music was still playing. He heard a scuffle of movement, before the girl called out: "What is it?"

"I want to talk to you," Rollison said, and pushed the door wide open.

She was sitting on the bed – not in it – wearing the trousers and the coat, the top of which was unbuttoned because the room was warm. She looked a little flushed, and her eyes were huge and a beautiful violet blue. The music was coming from the small radio at the side of the bed. A few cigarettes were there, too, and a tea-tray: obviously Jolly was giving her VIP treatment. The odd thing was that she looked almost contented, as if now that she was here she had no complaint. She did not smile at him, and was very wary; but she was not afraid of him, and that might be a pity.

"Hallo," Rollison greeted, amiably. "Enjoying yourself?"

"I insist on being allowed to go home," Kitty said with dignity. "You've no right to keep me here."

"Haven't I?" Rollison asked, and his smile had an edge. "I've a lot of rights that no one told you about, Kitty. Why did you drug yourself last night?"

She didn't answer.

Rollison went nearer to the bed and stood looking down at her, reminding himself that in her petite way she was as lovely a creature as he had ever seen. Lucky Cedric!

Or was he so lucky?

"Kitty," Rollison said. Now his voice was much softer and had a note of menace which he had well learned to acquire. "You released that man last night, and you took pills to make you sleep because he told you to. Why?"

"He made me!" She raised clenched hands. "I told you this last night. He made me do it, he said he will kill Cedric—"

"I don't believe it," Rollison retorted. "I don't believe that was the only hold he had over you. He was helpless, and couldn't do a thing. You knew that Cedric had come to see me, and believed that I could help him. You knew that Cedric had been kidnapped, and that the man could tell me where to find him—yet you let him go. Why?"

Her face was scarlet.

"You've no right to talk to me like this!"

"Those rights again," said Rollison, and swung round towards the door. "All right, you must have it your own way. You'll find an afternoon dress in that wardrobe, and some shoes that look as if they'll fit you. Get dressed. We're going out."

She gasped: "Where are we going?"

"To New Scotland Yard."

"No," she exclaimed, and scrambled off the bed and rushed towards him. "No, don't take me there; don't make me go to the police!"

She was really frightened by the prospect, and her fear told Rollison a great deal. Such fear of the police was abnormal, and he could think of at least one very good explanation: that she had a police record.

If she had, then there might be many explanations of why she had done what last night's prisoner had ordered.

Now he needed to see Grice again; but first he could make the girl talk, at least a little; unless her fear of the men who had taken her husband away was greater than the fear of the police.

He would soon find out.

Chapter Seventeen

Kitty Talks

Kitty Dwight was just in front of Rollison, clutching at his hands, her great eyes pleading. Her very beauty must have won her nearly everything she had ever desired, and she knew how to use it. Even now she might be trying to fool him by pretended fears; but he did not think so. Her body was too tense, her hands clenched too tightly.

"Kitty," he said softly, "what were you sent to prison for?"

She stood absolutely rigid, staring at him, looking like a doll, mouth fixed open, eyes rounded, clutched fists raised. It was easy to believe that she had stopped breathing. Then she backed away a pace, as if worked by clockwork, but did not move in any other way at all. He waited for the shock to ease, but it took a long time. The music changed tempo; a band was playing rock and roll, and it seemed so out of place and completely wrong in mood.

"No," Kitty breathed. "It's not true; they've lied to you, it's not true." And then, as if she did not know what she was saying, she added: "They promised never to tell anyone. They promised."

"What was it for, and when?" asked Rollison, gently. "No one need know unless you decide that it's best to tell Cedric."

She looked utterly lost and forlorn.

"No," she breathed. "Cedric mustn't know." There was a pause before she added: "They promised that they wouldn't tell anyone."

It would be pointless to try to persuade her that no one had told him; better, in fact, for her to think that her secret had been betrayed.

"Tell me what it was for," Rollison insisted.

She closed her eyes, and he remembered how effectively she could use those eyes. It seemed a long time before she spoke, and when she did it was in a husky, whispering voice.

"I—I took some clothes and cosmetics from the place where I worked."

"Where was that, Kitty?"

"Berridges."

Rollison had good reason to know that Berridges were well known for the severity of their discipline; no one there ever had a second chance, and perhaps that was understandable, for it was a big departmental store, and at the mercy of an unreliable staff.

"I was in the cosmetics department," Kitty told him, miserably. "A—a friend—a friend of mine was in lingerie. It—it looked so easy, and when she suggested it I—well, I just did it."

"How much were the things worth?"

"I couldn't be sure," answered Kitty Dwight. Suddenly her eyes seemed huge and round and luminous, as if this were the moment of her greatest plea. "It went on for nearly six months before we were found out. I'm not going to pretend it was just an impulse. I knew I shouldn't be doing it, but once it started it was ever so difficult to stop. I—I'd never been used to having enough money to buy everything I wanted, and I'd always lived in a back room and shared it with two cousins. Suddenly I was able to have a little room of my own, and Cora had a room in the same flat." Rollison did not stop her to ask if "Cora" was the girl with whom she had stolen these goods, for now she had started, words seemed to pour out of her. "I just couldn't give it up! Cora—Cora always sold the things. She had several boyfriends who bought them, but she was very strict with them, they never stayed the night. I didn't really *think* what I was doing; I kind of grew into thinking it was—was quite all right. Then one day I was stopped while leaving the shop."

She looked as if she could swoon with the recollection of that dread moment.

"Was Cora stopped, too?" inquired Rollison.

"Oh, yes," answered Kitty. "She was given two years' imprisonment, because it wasn't her first offence. I—I spent six months in prison. Every day was horrible. I'm not making that up! *Every* day was terrible, and sometimes I dream about it at night now. I came out of prison a year ago, and had nowhere to go and nothing to do, but— Cora's friends looked after me."

"The men who were at your flat last night?"

"Yes," said Kitty, and so simply explained almost everything that needed explanation. "They found me work as a photographer's model, and that was how I met Cedric. I knew I ought to tell him, but I daren't, because I was afraid that he wouldn't want to marry me. I simply couldn't give him up."

"Kitty," Rollison said softly, "how fond of Cedric are you?"

"I worship him," she declared, her voice vibrant with simplicity. "I would do absolutely anything for him. I'm terrified that he might find out about the past, and—and these men threatened to tell him, unless I did what they wanted. That's why I let the man go, and why I took the sleeping tablets." She closed her eyes again, and he thought that she looked very tired. "I didn't mean to tell you or anyone; I just prayed that everything would work out all right."

"I think perhaps it will," Rollison said. "Where is this photographer's studio?"

"In Crew Street, off the Edgware Road."

"Fine," said Rollison, and studied her closely, smiled a little, and said: "Now that I know all this, I'm as big a menace to you as the others, aren't I?"

"Yes."

"Who would you rather trust?"

"You," said Kitty, huskily. "That's if you'll help me, now that you know about my past."

"Kitty," said Rollison gently, "you made a fool of yourself and committed a crime, and you paid for it. That's over. Provided you don't let Cora or these friends of hers make you commit more crimes, you've nothing to worry about, and I'll help you all I can. A lot of my friends in the East End of London have spent years in jail for far worse crimes than yours."

"What?"

Rollison laughed.

"That's true, believe it or not! Have you any idea where Cedric is?"

"No."

"What else did these men want you to do?"

"They didn't want me to tell you anything about the studio, or about the past."

"I can understand that, too," said Rollison. "Do you think you could face them again?"

Kitty didn't answer, but just stared at him, and her eyes were asking "Why?"

"If I let you go, they'll pick you up," Rollison said. "I can have you followed, and find out where they take you. You must tell them that you didn't say a word to me about anything that matters; you just refused to talk. Afterwards you must take a big risk, Kitty."

"What risk?"

"You must tell them that if they don't let you know where Cedric is, you'll talk to me or to the police."

She caught her breath.

"They'd kill me if I did!"

"They might try to. I'd make sure they didn't. On the other hand, they might be so relieved that you haven't told me anything yet, that they would tell you where to find Cedric. They might even let you see him. Then you'd have to tell me, but that needn't come until later."

There was a long pause, in which neither of them moved. Then: "All right," Kitty said, very slowly. "I can see what you mean, and it's worth trying."

"That's fine!" It would be easy to marvel at this girl's courage, Rollison thought, unless she had fooled him – and he did not think she had. In any case he could soon find out if part of her story was true. "Kitty."

"Yes?"

"Do you know what these men want with Cedric?"

"No, I haven't the faintest idea," Kitty answered promptly. "I tried to make him tell me how it was they could frighten him so much, but he wouldn't talk about it. The awful thing was that these were friends of Cora's; in a way I'd let him in for it."

"He won't be frightened when this is over," Rollison said.

"Do you think you really can help?"

"Many more difficult situations have worked out happily ever after," Rollison answered brightly, "and these people aren't anything like as good as they think they are. Now get dressed, and be ready to leave in half an hour."

He went out before she could speak, and approached the door of Jolly's room. He hesitated, then opened it. A gust of heat-laden air struck him; it was already almost as hot as a Turkish bath. The prisoner was sitting just as he had been before, but his face was streaked with sweat which ran into his eyes and mouth, and he could not move his arms to wipe it off or help himself in any way. Rollison stared at him, seeing the red, puffy face, the greasy eyes, the physical distress: and he closed the door without a word.

Jolly was coming from the kitchen.

"Give him an hour, and then talk to him," Rollison said. "Just make him tell you who he works for, where the headquarters are, and where Dwight is."

"Very good, sir."

"I'm going to the Yard," Rollison said, "and—"

He broke off, for the telephone bell rang; there still wasn't time to breathe between one thing and another, and the ordinary day-to-day incidents of living became burdensome. He let Jolly answer, and hoped that it was a call about which he could take a message; but almost at once Jolly said: "I will find out if he is in. Hold on, please."

"Who is it?" asked Rollison.

"Miss Isobel Cole, sir."

"Oh," said Rollison. "All right, I'll talk to her." He took the receiver, greeted briskly: "Rollison speaking, Miss Cole," and heard the girl draw in her breath, as if now that she had plucked up courage enough to get him on the line, she found it difficult to speak. "How are you this morning?"

"Did you—did you see Bob?" Isobel burst out.

"Yes, last night."

"You are going to help him, aren't you?"

"I'll do everything I can."

"In—in spite of this other case that's in all the papers?" she demanded. It was easy to imagine her distress, and that of Mrs. Benning, too. "I know I've no right to expect you to concentrate just on Bob, but he didn't do it, Mr. Rollison, I'm sure he didn't do it."

"I'll prove he didn't, if that's true."

"You *will*, won't you?" she begged.

He thought of how much she and Kitty Dwight had in common, in spite of the gulf which now yawned between them. He could picture this girl's face, and the depth of her anxiety. He wanted to find some words of reassurance, but they were not easy.

He said: "I think this other case will be over in a day or so, and then I'll concentrate on Bob. I've made a start already."

"The thing that worries me—" Isobel began, and then broke off: and for the first time Rollison realised that she was not alone, for he distinctly heard another woman break in sharply. *"Don't say that!"* the speaker ordered, and he knew that Mrs. Benning was in the same telephone-box, still joined in the battle for her son.

"Say anything you like," Rollison invited.

"I can't help it," Isobel Cole cried. "I'm terrified in case you get killed! No one would be able to help Bob then."

"I've told you before, it would take more than a ducking to kill *him*," said Mrs. Benning, and her voice came more clearly; she had taken over the telephone. "I'm sorry, Mr. Rollison, but Isobel's quite overwrought. She'll be all right soon. Is there anything else that we can do?"

"Nothing at all, yet," Rollison reassured her. "I'll be in touch the moment I want anything from you."

"Well, then, good-bye," Mrs. Benning said.

When Rollison rang off, he was frowning at his Trophy Wall. He could hardly blame himself, yet he felt a sense of guilt at the unhappiness both the women were feeling, and the fact that he had really done nothing for them. Of course, he might get a break. After his appeal last night Ebbutt's men would do everything they could, but even Ebbutt himself had made the circumstances look blacker against young Benning. And the hope of results from the Salvation Army seemed very forlorn.

The telephone bell rang again.

"Rollison speaking."

"It is the secretary of the Northern London Hospital here," a man said, briskly. "I promised to keep you informed about Mr. Ebbutt's condition." There was a pause, and in it Rollison seemed to stop breathing, he was so afraid of what he might be told. Then the man went on: "There is no major change, and every few hours he remains the same are hours gained."

"Thanks," breathed Rollison, and added with an effort: "Thank you very much."

"Very glad to do anything I can for you, Mr. Rollison," the secretary said. "I've been reading about you since I was a boy."

"I hope you go on reading about me until you're an old man," rejoined Rollison. "Thanks again."

He felt in much better spirits when he rang off. He deliberated, decided that it would be wiser to see Grice than to telephone him, and that this was as likely a time to find him in his office as any. There had been a time when Grice had been out and about a great deal, but promotion held him more often to his desk.

He told Jolly that he would be back in about two hours, and went out. As he passed the door of Number 29, he thought of the bullet-mark which wasn't there, and the evidence that the chief purpose of that "attack" had been to frighten Cedric Dwight. Odd that the people now involved in this should once have been involved with the kind of larceny that the girl had described; in comparatively small crime.

Was it so small?

Pilfering was becoming worse and worse, in many phases of public life, and big departmental stores were more vulnerable than most. Not long ago he had been involved in a case where theft from a big wholesalers had reached vast proportions, and had led to murder and a campaign of violence greater than this one. There was a possibility that Kitty had been one of many girls who had been lured into stealing goods which were easy to sell: that for every one caught and sentenced, there might be ten still active and free. It could be a red herring, but it had to be considered.

He reached the mews where he kept his Rolls-Bentley. He had an arrangement with the mechanics at a small garage opposite to open the sliding doors and take the car out ready for him; and there it stood, massive and low slung, a beauty in twin-tone grey, always a sight which did him good. If the traffic wasn't too bad, he would be at the Yard in ten minutes. The essential thing was to find out why the police had been so helpful; whether in fact they knew anything which would enable him to understand the campaign against Cedric Dwight.

Then he saw the front nearside tyre was flat.

That happened so seldom that he was immediately suspicious and wary. He walked round the car, glancing at each tyre; only the one was down. The garage doors were wide open and two men were in sight, working; they would change the wheel for him in a minute or two, the fact that the car had had a puncture did not really matter, but the possibility that the tyre had been deflated deliberately, either to delay or to put him in danger, was sharp in his mind.

He saw no sign of other damage.

He called: "Nobby!" to the garage man at the bench, and then, to save time, went to the boot. He did not open it at first, for there might be a booby trap: it could have been done to make him open the door, and it would not be the first time that an explosive went off in an unsuspecting man's face. He stood to one side, as he inserted his key, turned it very slowly, and held his breath. Nothing happened, except that the chunky mechanic came up, briskly. "Lend me a long handled tool, will you?" Rollison asked. "The longer the better."

Nobby needed only a glance to know that Rollison was on edge. He hurried back to the garage and came carrying a long pole, with a curved hook at the end, the kind used for moving high windows.

"This do?"

"Fine, thanks," said Rollison. "Now stand at the front of the car, Nobby, and if I get blown to little pieces, tell the police."

He grinned tautly as he spoke, stood well to one side, put the hook under the handle of the boot, and gradually levered it up. He was half prepared for an explosion, and shaded his face with his left arm.

There was no explosion.

But there was a man in the boot.

Chapter Eighteen

Silent Fear

Now Rollison threw the boot lid up, handed the pole back to Nobby, and stepped right in front of the open boot. The man was heaped inside, and his coppery-coloured hair identified him at a glance, but did not say whether he was alive or dead.

This was Cedric Dwight.

If he were alive, would it make any sense?

Rollison did not ask himself how the boot had been forced; hardly thought of anything but the discovery, and fear that the youth was dead. Nobby had uttered a single exclamation, and been silent ever since. A car passed the end of the mews, and the other mechanic began to hammer some metal. Rollison moved forward and eased Dwight round, and would not have been surprised to see the evidence of murder on his face or on his head.

There was none.

His flesh was warm to the touch, too; if he were dead it had not been for long. Rollison took his wrist and felt his pulse. It was beating steadily, if a little faintly: as it would if he had been drugged. There was no sign at all of injury.

"Blimey!" Nobby said.

"Couldn't agree with you more," said Rollison. "Did you see anyone about the car?"

"No, sir, but I had to shut the place up for half an hour this morning; there was an emergency job."

"That was when they did this, then," Rollison mused. He leaned inside and lifted Dwight out; the man was a light weight. "Can I use a car to take him round to my flat, while you fix my nearside front wheel?"

"Pleasure, sir," said Nobby. "Take the Daimler; her ladyship never minds if we use it in an emergency. The ignition key's in the dash."

He stood aside, and then hurried to open the door of a stately old Daimler, so that Rollison could lift his burden in. Rollison dumped Dwight on the seat next to the driver's, and then took the wheel. He had not gone beyond pondering this new development, and the fact that he could not move at all without coming up against something which delayed him, or puzzled him, or alarmed him. He was more puzzled by this development than by anything else. He had taken it for granted that Dwight had been wanted by the men for some specific purpose. If that were so, why bring him back?

They were good, Rollison thought, uneasily; and they allowed a sense of humour some rein, which suggested overweening confidence.

Suppose they had got what they wanted from Dwight?

That seemed the most likely answer; and if they had, then Dwight should be able to talk. But not yet: he would be out for several hours, judging from appearances. Rollison felt a little bemused when he reached the front door of Number 22 and got out. He had hardly opened the other door when Wrightson came hurrying from the house, obviously on Jolly's instructions.

"Anythink up, Mr. Ar?"

"We've got a present," Rollison said. "Take this upstairs for me, will you?"

"Isn't that *Dwight*?"

"A present for Kitty," Rollison said, "but don't let her know about this yet. Tell Jolly to put Dwight in my bedroom and lock the door."

"How did you know where to find him?" marvelled Wrightson, and there was the look of hero-worship on his strong face.

Rollison grinned. "That's the nicest compliment I've had in years," he said. "But he was given to me, Percy; I didn't find him.

Jolly will be able to tell what's keeping him under the weather, and will call a doctor if necessary, but I don't think there'll be any need."

Wrightson grinned, lifted Cedric, and took him in. Two people on the other side of the road stared curiously, but showed no surprise; obviously they knew who lived on the top floor of that particular house. Rollison drove back to the garage, still trying to work the situation out, and more sure than ever that Grice would be able to tell him a great deal that mattered.

The Rolls-Bentley was ready, and Grice was in.

"Well," said Grice, after he had listened attentively, "they're certainly pushing you around, Rolly. Aren't you getting exhausted?"

"Only in body," said Rollison, virtuously. "The spirit is as resilient as ever. So are the suspicions. What are you up to, Bill?"

"*What* did you say?"

"The guileless air of candour doesn't sit well on you," said Rollison. "You're letting me get away with too much. Why?"

"You're dreaming."

"Bill," said Rollison firmly, "I think that you know what is behind all this, and for some reason you can't do much about it, so—"

"Oh, come," protested Grice, almost too smoothly. "We know you're good, but we haven't reached the stage when the Yard has to stand by and leave everything to you."

"That wasn't what I meant, and you know it," Rollison said. "What's ham-stringing you?"

"You're still dreaming."

"What did you find at Apex House last night?"

Grice said: "An empty safe, and everything else just as you left it. We've got the three men on a charge of burglary, but we can't prove that anything was actually stolen. We can send them down for six months or so, but that's about all. No one was hurt, nothing really taken away, and they've no records."

"Ever heard of Kitty Dwight?"

"I know what you mean," said Grice. "We found the inevitable crop of fingerprints at the apartment, and gave them a routine check. A Kathleen Forsyth, convicted eighteen months ago for stealing from her employers, served six months' imprisonment, and thereafter kept her nose clean, as far as we know—but they were her prints last night, and there was a photograph of her in the flat, too."

"Are you trying to say that you didn't know Dwight was married?"

"We didn't know until to-day," Grice said firmly. "They were married in a Registry Office, and we didn't think they'd worried about marriage lines. I wonder if Dwight knew what he was marrying."

"She says he didn't," Rollison told him.

"So you managed to make her talk," said Grice, and went on quickly: "What about the man you're holding at the flat? Have you got anything out of him?"

"No."

"You're slipping."

"Bill," said Rollison, very softly, "you're much too suave and calm this morning. Presumably you think you've got me on the end of a piece of string. What is it all about?"

"If I knew anything, I would tell you," Grice said.

"Provided it didn't break regulations."

"Naturally."

"Has Dwight got a record?" Rollison demanded, abruptly.

"No."

"How prominent are his relatives?"

"Fairly prominent industrial and commercial bankers," Grice answered, "but not prominent enough to make us go warily."

"I still don't get it," said Rollison.

"For almost as long as I've been at the Yard, you've been complaining that we didn't give you enough rope," Grice said, with a smile. "You've complained bitterly at times that if you were able to take the law into your own hands more you could use short cuts forbidden to us; and that if we'd just sit back and leave it to you, you would often be able to present us with a prisoner on a plate. That's true, isn't it?"

"A qualified yes."

Grice grinned. "It doesn't need qualifying. That's what you've meant, even if you haven't actually said it. And I've often agreed with you, although the great men at the top haven't. A good amateur who'll take chances can do a lot of things quicker than we can. Now here's a case where we're not using all the regulations to hold you up. You can go on at your own pace, and get results as quickly as you like. That's what you've always wanted, and now you complain because of it. Why aren't you more consistent, Rolly?"

"I give up," Rollison said, and rose to his feet. "Found anything else about the raid on Ebbutt's place?"

"The Razzo boys were paid two hundred pounds to wreck it, and they were told to follow the two men who attacked Ebbutt," Grice answered, no longer smiling. "They say that the man whose neck was broken paid them the money and they didn't see the second man closely, so they can't identify him. A typical cover-up, and I don't think we'll be able to uncover it."

"Did they know why Ebbutt's place was to be wrecked?"

"They said they hadn't any idea."

"Do you think it could have been to try to stop Ebbutt's men from helping me?"

"Obviously it is possible, but it's only guesswork," Grice said. He glanced down at some documents on his desk, and a new, grimmer note entered his voice. "We've more information about young Benning which you can have, Rolly. It isn't good. We've tried five of the pubs where he met Marjorie Fryer, and in each case he left first, and she afterwards showed the money which he'd given her."

"Was he seen handing it to her?"

"I couldn't produce an eye-witness, but there's such a thing as circumstantial evidence," Grice said. "That's one of the things that we poor police have to take into account. We can get a conviction against Benning without the slightest trouble, and I think you're wasting your time on him."

"Have you checked if any motor-cyclist was about when the Fryer girl was killed?"

"We haven't traced any or heard of any."

"Sure that a man on a motor-cycle didn't kill her and nip off?"

"If you can prove one did, I'd be astonished," Grice said.

"I think we'll prove it," declared Rollison, but he felt frustrated; felt sure that there was more behind the attitude of the police than he could fathom.

The one possible source of information now were Ebbutt's men.

He left Grice and drove along the Embankment to Blackfriars and then through the crowded City streets. A heavy bank of clouds was blowing up, and there was quite a wind; it might blow up into a bad storm. It was beginning to rain, big, heavy spots, when he pulled up outside the gymnasium. Usually it was almost deserted at this hour of the day, for most of Ebbutt's boys were part-timers, who trained in the evening. Now there were five or six small cars, a dozen motor-cycles, and as many cycles outside; he had never seen more people here during the day. He heard a noise of hammering, too, and as he hurried from the Rolls-Bentley, knowing that children were already rushing up to see it, he heard a man calling out: "Careful with it. Don't drop it."

He reached the doorway.

Thirty men or more were inside the big, low-roofed building, and every one seemed to be in a frenzy of activity. Men were hammering, banging, sawing, screwing-up. The wall-bars on one side were repaired and back in place. The vaulting horses were acquiring new legs. The punch-balls were without their deflated tops, but the stands looked sound again. Five men were rolling out a stretch of canvas, for the ring itself; the torn and ripped canvas had already been taken away.

Nothing would do Ebbutt more good than the knowledge of this; and nothing did Rollison more good than the sight of it. He stood and watched, exhilarated, touched by the qualities in these men who were so rough and ready, so crude and so often rude.

Then he saw Lil Ebbutt, in her uniform and wearing her hat on the back of her head, a pencil poking from her grey hair, standing in the doorway of the office and waving across at him; and smiling.

Sam, whose other name was Mitchell, came across, grinned, said: "How's this for a bit of all right?" and added: "Lil wants you. She's picked up a bit about young Benning from one of the Army lassies. Never can tell, can you?"

He went back to his task, of screwing in parallel bars, while Rollison pushed his way across towards Lil, marvelling that she should smile and have such courage – and that she might have hope not only for herself but for another woman.

Chapter Nineteen

Army Lass

"I wasn't doing no good at the 'ospital," said Lil, lapsing into her broadest Cockney. "The nurses was doing all they could. I thought I was more use 'ere, Mr. Ar, and I must say that this 'as done me a world of good. Never would 'ave believed these men would put their backs into a job like this. Love your neighbour in practice, that's what it is. I always told Bill 'e was wasting 'is time with a crowd of lazy loafers, but after all this—well, a woman's got every right to change 'er mind, 'asn't she?"

"If she's got the grace to, Lil."

"Funny thing," Ebbutt's wife went on, and there was a suspicion of moisture at her eyes, "but until you nearly lose someone, you don't even evalooate them properly. I've always loved Bill, of course, but the times I've tried to make 'im give up this gym, *and* the pub, and make 'im take up sunning I said was respectable. I'll tell you one thing, Mr. Ar: I'll never do it again. I was telling the General about it last night; 'e come to see me at the 'ospital. Spiritual pride, he called it." Something had brought Lil up sharply to a realisation of the broadness of her speech, and she became more cautious and careful, and so a little less natural. "If there's as much good as this in this crowd of men, God wouldn't want me to stop Bill from knowing them."

Rollison grinned. "Nor would Bill!"

Lil surprised him by bursting out with laughter.

"Now I don't want none of that, Mr. Ar! If you got down on your knees and prayed a bit more often it wouldn't do you no harm. Do you know what I've found out this morning?"

"No, Lil."

"Come in here," she ordered, and took his arm and led him into the small office. On the littered desk was a pair of steel-rimmed spectacles, one of the arms bound round with cotton; these were Bill's, as he had put them down last night. His books were spread out on the desk. He had a spidery handwriting, and often used pencil when ink would have shown up much more boldly, but the general effect was neat enough. "I always thought he was paying these men to hang about and do nothing but try to break a man's nose," Lil went on. "What do I find, Mr. Ar?"

He wanted to know what she had found out about Benning, but did not try to force the question then.

"What, Lil?"

"I find that there's a list as long as your arm of people he's helping—seven women get money from him whose men are in prison to my certain knowledge. Most of these chaps don't get the money for themselves; he gives it to them to take to people suffering hardship. Did you know, Mr. Ar?"

"I knew a lot about it, Lil."

"I come across some very interesting entries in a bank book," went on Lil. "Every now and again there's a credit of a few hundred pounds—twice it's as high as seven hundred and fifty. It's not from Bill's own account. I know he makes money from stocks and shares and things, and buys and sells land, but those accounts are all in the book, for the income-tax people. These are marked 'Anonymous Donor', and they all go into what he calls his Hard Cases account. Do you know the name of the anonymous donor, Mr. Ar?"

Her eyes were very bright.

"Lil," said Rollison obtusely, "what's this about a message from a lassie about young Benning?"

"I thought as much," said Lil, slowly. "Mr. Ar is seenonymous with Mr. Anonymous." She looked a little bewildered, as if she thought there was something wrong with the phrase, but went on without a pause: "I don't mind admitting that there's been times when I thought that a gentleman like you, with your education, ought to know better than to hobnob with these types, and always start worrying Bill to find you men to help you. But I can see what it is now. You and Bill have a lot in common, haven't you?"

"A lot, Lil."

"This Bob Benning," Lil announced, abruptly. "Some of my Army friends made inquiries, like you asked. Bob was in the Army once, or jolly near it."

"Your Army?" Rollison was surprised, until he recalled the expression on Bob Benning's face; he wasn't really surprised.

"It's the only one worth talking about," declared Lil, with a flash of her usual spirit; for years she had been the most intolerant person in the East End. "The Army never gives up; you oughter know that. If there's the slightest hope of getting a young man or a girl to join, we keep after them. That Isobel Cole, now, she's another—just on the fringe, you might say; she thinks she'd like to join, but she can't make herself give *everything*."

"What can you tell me, Lil?"

"You reminded us how often our lassies go into the pubs with the *War Cry*," said Lil, "but probably you don't know how many of us go in for a lemonade just so's to find out what's going on. Sometimes they can stop a young man or a girl from falling too far down the slippery slopes. Once they're on the way it's hard to stop them, but if you can get at 'em before they really start, then you've got a chance."

"No one ever fooled you for long," Rollison remarked.

"I'm beginning to wonder," said Lil. "Well, this Bob Benning was one we've bin watching."

Rollison felt his heart begin to beat faster. There might be much more in this than he had hoped at first. The Army was tenacious and the Army was thorough. If there were one or two Army witnesses in the box on Bob Benning's behalf it would be a great help for the defence.

"Go on," he urged.

"Well, this girl Marjorie Fryer followed Bob around. He tried to get away from her, but she just wouldn't keep away. She kept asking him to buy her drinks, and now and again he did, more's the pity. Sometimes she invited him to bed with her. No point in mincing matters," Lil went on, brusquely, "and that's the truth. I dunno whether you realise it, but some people get *worse* when anyone is trying to do them a bit of good. An extra bit of nastiness seems to come out. Marjorie Fryer couldn't stand the Army. If any one of us got near her she would say all kinds of things, and use dreadful language, as if she wanted to get under our skin. Not that there's any fear of that; we don't send anyone who's sensitive out to the pubs," Lil asserted. "Two or three times she was heard talking really bad to young Bob Benning, though."

"Did he respond?" asked Rollison.

"Mr. Rollison, every time our people went out and followed them," said Lil. "If he'd looked like going with her, they would have remonstrated with him, and tried to draw him back from the yawning pit. Well, he never did. He always went off on his own."

Rollison exclaimed eagerly: "Even on the night of the murder?"

"Yes."

"Lil, you'll never know how much this means," said Rollison, and actually gripped her arm. "Who followed them that night?"

"Jane Martin's husband," Lil answered. "They live at 91, The Green; you know where that is as well as I do. I saw Jane this morning—she was on her way to the mission—and I asked her. Yes, she said, her Fred had told her about it. Fred's a long-distance lorry driver, and he went off early the morning after, so he didn't know anything about the murder. You can take it from me, Mr. Ar, that he's the witness you want." Lil gave a swift, bright smile, looked up into his face and said: "I'm nearly as good as Bill, aren't I, Mr. Ar?"

"Lil," said Rollison, fervently, "you're better. When is Fred Martin due home?"

"Should be there now; he's only had a Birmingham job," answered Lil. "He usually gets back to the depot about two o'clock, Jane said, and knocks off right away—three days on duty, one day off; that's how he works."

"Thanks, Lil," Rollison said. "I'll go and have a talk to him."

"And don't forget to tell young Bob Benning who told you," Lil said. "If that boy's got any sense he'll join up with us and bring the girl along, too. That Isobel's a bit too fond of make-up and dancing, but that's natural enough in the young."

"The Army might be the making of her," Rollison said solemnly. "Lil, when did you last hear about Bill?"

"Just before you come in, when Mr. Jolly telephoned. Bill's going to pull through," the woman added quietly. "Last night I nearly gave up hope, but this morning I feel different. It's like a Phoenix rising from the ashes," she added, and looked out of the open doorway. "That's right, isn't it? I don't believe God would be so cruel as to stop my Bill from seeing all this. Mind you, he'll have to go slow, Mr. Ar. You off to see Fred right away?"

"I can't get there fast enough," Rollison said.

He gripped her hands, and then turned and went out, seeing that the work was going on with just as much vigour as before. Nothing could be more heartening; and nothing pleased him more than the news he would soon have for Isobel and Mrs. Benning.

He remembered Fred Martin, whom he had met at Lil's flat from time to time, when she held meetings there. A big, burly, hard-voiced man, he had seemed the type likely to burst out in a torrent of foul language at the slightest provocation. It had been startling to see him blowing a trombone lustily to the glory of God.

What a witness Fred would be!

Fred Martin was a little late on the road that day, but he did not hurry, because he followed only one rule of the road: it was as safe as sitting in your own front room provided you didn't try to go too fast. He was not only big, burly, and tough, but he was placid. The one emotion which seemed to spark in him was for hymn-singing and trombone playing; those really woke him up. Otherwise he moved slowly, acted calmly and cautiously, and simply did his job. He was a good driver, although not outstanding. Sometimes he exasperated his employers, a large firm of grocers and provision merchants with shops all over the country, because he was inclined to be late; not lazy, just careful.

He ran into the storm on the other side of Watford, and as the weather had been so dry for the past ten days, there was a lot of oil on the road. So he slowed down. The rain was very heavy, his windscreen wipers squeaked as they moved, cars passed, splashing muddy water over the windshield. At least it wasn't cold.

Then, in the teeming rain, he saw a man and a girl waving him down, obviously hoping for a lift. In dry weather he would have hesitated, but in a storm like this it was only Christian charity to stop and let them take shelter. Once they were in, he would take them as near their destination as he could. There was plenty of room in the cabin. He slowed down, and stopped right opposite the couple. The man was of medium height, wiry looking, with dark hair streaming with water which ran down his face. The girl had a plastic hood over her head and much of her face, and he could not see what she was like.

One never knew, thought Fred Martin, but there might be the beginning of a conversion here. You never knew what prompted you to stop, or when an opportunity would be thrust in your hands. The difficulty was to recognise it when it came. It would take an hour to get to London, and a lot could be done in an hour.

"Hop in," he invited, and the man climbed up, surprising Fred, because he had expected the girl to come first. "Okay, Ivy," he called. "I'll be seeing you." He slammed the door, and splashed Fred with the fine rain from his raincoat. "My girl's got to get back to work," he said. "Thanks for the lift."

"Welcome," said Fred, and was disappointed, because women were usually more interested in talk about religion; and this man did not look as if he would ever be very impressed. But one never could tell, Fred soothed himself, and drove for a few minutes in silence.

Then they reached The Hill.

It wasn't really a steep one, and drivers on this road called it The Hill because it was the only one for a long way. Here and there it was quite steep, but it was the long climb on the way out of London which made it a feature of the drive to Watford and the North. The rain was teeming down. There was little traffic on the road, partly because at this time of day traffic was always light, and partly because of the rain; several cars were drawn up under trees. There was a sudden flash of lightning, and Fred found himself thinking that the drivers of those cars ought to avoid trees.

He slowed down, to change gear, at the top of the hill.

Then he felt a sharp pressure at his neck, turned in surprised alarm, and saw the eyes of his passenger close to his. He raised his left hand off the wheel, and involuntarily his foot came off the clutch. In the same instant he felt the great lorry with its heavy load gathering speed in the lashing rain; and he felt the pressure at his neck, at his windpipe, increased.

He couldn't breathe.

He was being choked; and if he took his hands off the wheel he would lose control of the lorry. He knew great fear. He put his foot on the brake, and the lorry began to slow down, but the pressure at his throat increased, and the man had his wrist on the wheel so that he could not move it.

Soon the man thrust his head back against the wood behind him, then put on the hand-brake, and opened the door. Fred could do nothing, he was in such pain, but he saw the man climb out while the lorry was crawling; then saw him lean inside and release the hand-brake.

The man vanished as the lorry gathered speed.

As Fred tried desperately to save himself and to grip the brakes and hold the wheel, he saw another lorry loom up out of the rain. He just managed to press on the horn, heard it blaring its warning; then the other van seemed to come back and hit him.

He felt an awful pain in his head.

Chapter Twenty

"Accident"

"It's a funny thing," said Jane Martin, a merry-eyed woman in the middle forties, "but Fred's usually home from the Birmingham run long before this. He won't be long now, Mr. Ar; I'm sure of that."

"Tell him I'd like to see him, will you?" asked Rollison. "I'll be back by half-past four."

"He'll be in—never goes out after a run," Martin's wife declared. "He says all he wants to do is take it easy for a couple of hours. Can't have much more than that to-night; it's band practice."

"I don't promise to come to that," said Rollison.

He was a little uneasy, because this delay was the kind of coincidence which could be the herald of trouble. He had not wanted to give Jane the slightest cause for alarm, so had not told her that he was going to the big yard where the lorry would be unloaded, to find out if there was any news of Fred. It was close to the docks, and when he was stopped at the gates by an elderly gatekeeper who seldom had Rolls-Bentleys in the grime and confusion here, he saw twenty or thirty lorries backed against loading platforms, men busy, machines working, and in the distance the docks from which much of the food was unloaded. He saw the derricks of three ships, and heard the rattle of cranes.

"Do you know if Fred Martin's back?" he asked the gatekeeper.

"No, sir. He's in Truck 36; should have been in at two o'clock, and it's now half-past four."

The gatekeeper was frowning, probably because he was sure that he had seen this man before, but did not know where.

"Have you any idea how far he is on the road," Rollison asked.

"They might have some news at the office," answered the gatekeeper. "I haven't heard anything. It's okay to go through if—Cor!—aren't you—"

Rollison said, smiling absently: "Yes, I'm Rollison." He was worried, in spite of his smile. "Thanks, I'll go and find out."

He drove through the gateway, knowing that the man was staring after him and gaping. The huge lorries all glistened from the afternoon storm, although the sun was shining now. He reached a door marked: *"Office, Report Here"*, and tapped on the door and stepped inside. The moment he did so, he sensed trouble, and it did him no good at all. A tall, very thin girl, so flat-breasted that she hardly seemed mature, was standing by a desk. A short, fat man with a face like a monkey sat with his hand at a telephone. A boy, with ginger hair and freckles, looked scared.

The monkey-like man said: "Good—good afternoon, sir," as if he felt sure that this was someone from the management. "He—he's dead."

Rollison made himself ask: "Who's dead?"

"Why, Fred Martin, of course. Didn't you—" The man broke off and peered, as if short-sightedly, at Rollison; and then he stood up quickly. "I'm sorry, I thought you were Mr. Lennox; he said he would come over. There was an accident on the hill, sir. Terrible. He was the most careful of drivers, Fred was. I can hardly believe that Fred would die in an accident."

A tall, middle-aged man came in, and stopped abruptly.

"Did you say Fred Martin is *dead*?" he demanded.

"I can't believe it," Jane Martin said, almost stupidly. "There must be some mistake. *My* Fred's not dead." All the merriment had gone out of her eyes, and she stood motionless by the fireplace of her parlour, with its polished furniture, its sepia photographs, its Victorian bric-a-brac; and Fred's trombone in its long, shabby black case. She was very plump and rather pigeon-breasted, and now she was pressing a hand into her plump bosom. Two neighbours, each from the Army, were in the room with her and Rollison. "There must be some mistake," she repeated drearily. "He was the most careful driver in the world. He always said he would rather be an hour late, or a day if it came to that, rather than take chances. It must be a mistake. My Fred *can't* be dead."

There were two men with Rollison, dressed in the familiar blue uniform, and with the Salvation Army printed on the bands of their hats. They had driven with him to the morgue at Watford, and now they looked upon the cold face of their dead colleague. The Chief Inspector of the local police looked questioningly at each in turn, and each nodded and turned away, one too distressed to speak, the other saying in a hoarse voice: "It's Fred Martin all right, no doubt about that." So the identification was made formally, and they were led out.

Rollison saw a plump, ruddy-cheeked man in the Chief Inspector's office, and was introduced to him as Dr. Campbell.

"I haven't had time to do an autopsy yet, of course," said the pathologist, "but—at your request, I understand—I've come down from London to have a look at the body. There are no outward signs which are not quite consistent with this kind of accident. He obviously lost control going downhill."

"Brakes?" asked Rollison, of the Chief Inspector, and he knew that both men could see how shaken he was, and was grateful that they showed no resentment at his brusqueness.

"We'll have a quick look, but there seems to be nothing wrong. It was raining heavily at the time, and the road was greasy. The driver of the lorry in front said that he was having difficulty and was looking for a place to pull in. I should say that the driver lost control and didn't see the lorry in front because of the rain. Visibility was down to twenty or thirty yards."

"I don't believe that Fred Martin would take the slightest risk," insisted the Salvation Army major.

"It's amazing how often the best driver has a momentary lapse and gets away with it," the pathologist remarked. "I'm going to get busy now. Will you wait, Mr. Rollison, or shall I telephone you—or send a message through the Yard?"

"If you'll call me I'll be grateful," Rollison said.

Grice was still in his office, taking full advantage of the fact that his wife was away, and doing what he always enjoyed most: working. He seemed slightly older and rather less sure of himself as he looked at Rollison, shortly after seven-thirty that night – little more than twenty-four hours since Rollison had come here to see him about Dwight.

"The facts speak for themselves," he said quietly. "I tell you that I've had Campbell's autopsy report by telephone. There is absolutely nothing at all to suggest foul play. No bruises in unusual places, just a bump on the back of the head where Martin was jolted against the back of his driving-cabin, and a badly smashed forehead when he went forward. The lacerations, cuts, and bruises are all commensurate with the smash. It's no use being obstinate about it, Rolly. He died in an accident after losing control of the lorry."

"If you'd told me that he'd had a heart attack I might have believed you," Rollison said bleakly. "It wasn't an accident, Bill."

"Just because—" Grice began.

"Bob Benning didn't go away with that girl. Martin told his wife enough to make that clear. Hearsay isn't evidence, but Martin could have given evidence to prove that Benning didn't follow Marjorie Fryer from the pub when she was killed. Now a key witness is dead of violence."

"There's the autopsy report. There's the official police report on the condition of the brakes. There's nothing at all to suggest anything more than an unusual accident at a time when conditions for driving were bad."

"Bill," said Rollison, stonily, "Benning didn't kill the Fryer girl, and this man wasn't killed in an accident. I've checked everything possible about his habits, his mood, his caution. He simply isn't the man to take the slightest chance."

"If anything were the matter with the brakes I might say there was something in the argument," Grice interrupted, testily. "But there's nothing at all."

"Bill—"

"Rolly, there isn't a thing I can do."

"Bill, that boy could spend all his life in jail because you're being stubborn. It will cause you some extra trouble, and perhaps make a couple of men stay on overtime, and it may make the Yard's name mud. All right. It might save the boy, too. If the brakes are all right, if nothing is mechanically wrong, then Fred Martin wasn't alone in the cabin."

"Oh, nonsense!"

"Telephone Watford," Rollison urged. "Ask them to question everyone who was on that road yesterday. Have a radio and television request put out for information from anyone who saw the lorry. If there was a passenger—"

"There isn't the slightest justification for it!"

"Do it, Bill," Rollison urged. "Make sure you don't have this on your conscience."

"It simply isn't justifiable. The Commander and the Assistant Commissioner wouldn't authorise an approach to the BBC or independent television."

"Bill," said Rollison, almost savagely, "I have a lot of friends. I haven't had to pull that kind of string to make you do something for a long time, but if necessary I will. If the appeal isn't in the night's news, I'll start from the House of Lords and work downwards. You could do this on your own authority and apologise afterwards if it wasted time. You might even pretend that you thought of it yourself. We want to know if anyone was in the cab of Martin's lorry yesterday."

Grice said: "It's not possible. Let's drop the subject. Have you talked to Dwight yet?"

"I've hardly seen him."

"I'm told he's back at your flat."

"Yes," said Rollison, "and reunited with his Kitty. Jolly couldn't keep them apart. I talked to Jolly on the telephone, and Dwight won't say a word about what happened to him. Apparently he seemed as frightened as ever. What made you so co-operative over that and so stubborn over the other?"

Grice said: "I've talked to the A.G. this afternoon, and there are one or two things I can tell you. For the past twelve months we've been worried by reports of a gang operating a series of thefts. Sometimes they're from shops—like Kitty Dwight's—sometimes they're smash-and-grab, sometimes they're post-office hold-ups, sometimes straightforward burglaries. They last for about a week. You've often seen stories about them, and you thought the same as we did, at first: that it's a case of follow-my-leader; there always has been a crop of the same kind of crime, and it dies down. We fooled ourselves with that one," went on Grice, "but gradually we picked up reports which made us wonder whether we were right. The description of the men was always remarkably the same—well built, medium-sized men, rather ordinary to look at, and very fit. Whenever they got into any kind of difficulty they were always able to fight their way out of it. They were highly mobile—using motor-cycles which looked old but had great power. We caught several men on the crimes, but none admitted that they were associated with anyone else, and we couldn't prove that they were. But these men we caught were all very much alike in build and behaviour, they all wore dark clothes, they all had empty pockets. Five of them are serving sentences for different crimes at this moment."

Rollison, standing by Grice's desk, was very still.

"They were similar type of men to those you found at Apex House," Grice went on. "They will never talk. It wasn't until we learned that one of them had drugged himself that we realised you were involved in this inquiry—because all of them have had morphia pills, enough to put them out for twenty-four hours, enough to kill them if they wanted to die. That was the one connecting link, and we've been working on it. Then there was this case of Cedric Dwight. Everything I told you about him is true. He has had these illusions. His family has consulted psychiatrists about him. There was absolutely no reason to believe that he was in any danger, but when you told me about the man on the old motor-cycle, I took a deeper interest."

"Ah," said Rollison, owlishly.

"Then you were attacked over there," went on Grice, pointing out of the window to the sunlit Thames. "I knew at once that you were on to this particular job. What I didn't believe was that you knew nothing about it. I thought you realised just what you were after, and were trying to dig information from us that would help. So I played dumb. It's no use asking me how big or how widespread these crimes have been," Grice went on quite briskly. "They may have been organised for years; they may run into hundreds of thousands of pounds. We don't know: we do now know, thanks to you, that they're after Dwight. The A.G. and the Commander agreed with me that it was better to let you see if you could find out the truth, rather than let us tackle Dwight and his wife. This is a job where you might get the truth quicker than we could. And there's one interesting factor: although Dwight's been terrified, and in spite of his wife's fears, and the volume of crimes, there has never been a murder: violence, sometimes, but never murder. See what you can find out about it, Rolly."

Rollison stared out into the shimmering Thames, seeing the odd car pass, and the river-boats, and reminding himself of all the things of life that Martin had lost: and which Bob Benning might lose.

"Bill," he said, "put out those S.O.S. calls on the radio and television to-night, and I'll work on the Dwights. Refuse to put them out, and I shall tell the Dwights that I can't help them, and refer them to you."

He moved towards the door.

Grice said: "You're the most obstinate man I know."

Now Rollison could hardly wait for the nine o'clock news, which would tell him whether or not he had won the day.

But there was plenty to do. He checked over all the incidents of both the Benning and the Dwight case, and for a while seemed to be almost in a trance. What had he left undone? And what had he missed? If he could only see it, there was the answer to most of the problems.

Sam telephoned from the gymnasium.

"Anything you want, Mr Ar?" he enquired.

"Send some men to relieve Percy Wrightson," Rollison said, "and have Isobel Cole and Mrs. Benning watched closely, Sam."

"Strewth! No danger to them, is there?" Sam demanded.

"Better be safe than sorry," Rollison said.

He was smiling rather grimly when he rang off.

Chapter Twenty-One

Nine O'clock News

Rollison's flat was very quiet.

Percy Wrightson had gone home to see his wife. Two of Ebbutt's men were in the street, and another in the kitchen. Jolly was at some mysterious business in his workroom. So far as Rollison knew, Kitty Dwight was sitting in the armchair in the spare room, with the radio playing softly, books and magazines by her side, and her unconscious husband in bed. Rollison saw that it was five to nine, got up, and went to the spare room. He saw the girl glance round, recognised the start of fear which was never far away from her.

"Is he awake yet?"

"*No,*" she whispered.

Rollison went across to the bed, and Kitty stood up, looking as if she wanted to stop him, yet not daring to say a word. Rollison raised Dwight's right eyelid, and saw that the pupil was still small, although not so tiny. The indications were that he would soon start slipping out of unconsciousness into natural sleep; then it would be all right to wake him.

"I'll see him as soon as he comes round," Rollison said in his normal speaking voice.

"All right," Kitty whispered.

Was she scared of her husband or simply terrified of what might happen when he found out the truth about her past? He did not dwell on that, but went back to his room. The erstwhile prisoner was still in the hot room, as adamant as he had ever been.

Rollison turned the radio until it was quite loud.

He stood by the Trophy Wall, playing with the noose which had once choked the life out of a man, and the trophies of his chases were by his side. He was thinking of Fred Martin's death, and the ugliness of it, and the fact that he had prompted the Salvation Army people to make the inquiries. It was useless to tell himself that as soon as Fred had reached home and learned what had happened to Benning, he would have gone to the police – and that his attackers, knowing that, would have tried to stop him anyhow. He, Rollison, had been the direct instrument of the Army's inquiry: and so he had been responsible for a good man's death.

The thought haunted him.

The news signal came. He sat on the edge of the desk, took out some papers, and began to run through them: the list of friends and relations which the Bennings had given him. He knew them off by heart. The announcer talked of international tensions, a by-election, a Chinese flood disaster, in his steady, detached voice. Rollison picked up a newspaper which had a photograph of Isobel Cole in it. She was as pertly pretty as any picture; and that quirk of thought did not even make him smile.

There was a slight pause in the flow of words from the loudspeaker, and then the announcer said: "And here is a police message. At about 2.15 this afternoon, on the hill leading from the north to Watford, two lorries collided and a driver of one was killed, the driver of the other suffering facial and leg injuries. The police are anxious to interview anyone who saw the accident, and also anyone who was on that particular stretch of road between one forty-five and two-fifteen. Anyone who may be able to help is asked to communicate with New Scotland Yard, telephone number Whitehall 1212."

Rollison moved and switched off.

"Thanks, Bill," he said.

He went into the room where Jolly was busy, and told him. Jolly, at his bench, said quietly that he was very glad indeed; Jolly knew quite well what particular kind of hell Rollison was living through, although he did not refer to it.

"Now I'm going to try the prisoner," Rollison said. "If he won't talk this time—"

The man was sitting back in the chair, exhausted. He actually looked thinner. The room was not so viciously hot, but was still very hot indeed. The bars of three electric fires glowed. The man moved sluggishly when the door opened, and then started up. Rollison stood over him, and knew that he must exert any pressure and use any force to make this man talk of what he knew; but unless the man talked now, how could he be made to break down?

Rollison said roughly: "You think it's been hot, but we've only just started to warm up. I've news for you." His voice was iron hard and his expression bleak; and he saw what he thought was fear in the eyes of the other man, the first suggestion of a crack. "A friend of mine was murdered this afternoon. Understand that? I don't care what happens to you, I don't care how rough I have to be. I mean to find out who did it, and what this is all about."

It was the other case, of course; there had been no murder in the Dwight case, only violence and the threat of violence. But just as the Dwight case had got in the way of his investigation into the Benning case, so he could use what had happened in one to press forward with the other. They were almost the same in his mind now – a "double" in which the emphasis had switched during those awful minutes when he had learned what had happened to Fred Martin.

"I'll give you two minutes to make up your mind," he said, roughly. "Who do you work for? Who sent you here?"

The man stared at him, and Rollison saw that his lips were quivering, sensed that this was the moment he had been waiting for. He saw the sweat gathered like a pool round the other's bloodshot eyes, saw the pallor of his skin, knew how awful he felt, knew that the heat method had worked: and all that he had to find out now was whether this man knew anything that mattered.

He licked his lips.

"Gim—gimme some water," he muttered. "Water."

"Get some water, Jolly," Rollison ordered.

"Very good, sir."

The man stared into Rollison's eyes, trembling from head to foot. Rollison moved to him, cut the cords at the arms of the chair, bent down and cut the cords from the wrists. He said: "I can fasten them again."

Jolly came in, and the man's eyes turned towards the small glass of water as if it were a mountain of gold. Rollison took the glass. The man tried to stretch out his hand for it, but there was no strength in his arm. Jolly seemed to be breathing very softly; as if he, too, knew that this was the vital moment.

"Who do you work for? Who sent you here," demanded Rollison.

The man said: "It was Ivy; that's all I can tell you. It was Ivy." His voice croaked; he tried to stretch forward again, but could not. "It was Ivy; Ivy always gives the messages. I mu—must have a drink, I must—"

Rollison held the glass to his lips, let him sip, saw the frenzy in his eyes. He did not think that he would continue to be obstinate now that the crack had started. He gave him two minutes to let the water soak into his parched mouth, then took the glass away, and asked: "Who is Ivy?"

"She—she always gives us our orders," the man exclaimed. "She's the contact with—with the boss. It's no use asking who he is; I don't know. I'll tell you everything I do know; I can't stand the heat any longer; I can't stand it. Take me out, and I'll tell you everything I know."

"Come on, Jolly," Rollison said.

He took one arm, Jolly took the other, and they helped the prisoner along the passage and into the big, cool room. They set him in one of the armchairs in which Mrs. Benning and Isobel had sat only a day before. He looked as if he would collapse. Jolly brought a towel and dabbed his face and forehead, and brought in another glass of water. Then, unostentatiously, Jolly switched on a tape recorder which stood on Rollison's desk. It was working when the prisoner began to talk.

Grice, sitting in the room facing the Trophy Wall, listened as the tape recorder was played back. There was the prisoner's croaking voice, his obvious fear, his apparent collapse. It was hard to believe that a man could talk as he talked without telling the truth, for his voice made it obvious that there was no courage left in him.

The wheels stopped turning as the voice faded out.

"So there's a lot of your story," Rollison said, softly. "He's one of a group of thirty or forty men, all trained in most kinds of crime. They're all ex-fighting men, all about the same age—the early thirties—and part of the contract is to keep fit. They get a steady two thousand pounds a year each, basic, and ten per cent of the proceeds of whatever they help to steal. They're told what to do and where to go, and they're told to take these morphia tablets if they're caught; and with the morphia there's a mixture of a tranquillising drug which means that when they come out of unconsciousness they're not worried, and they can resist questioning easily. Very easy, and very clever. They always get their instructions from a woman. Some time ago it was a woman named Cora Dantry—Kitty Dwight's friend. Now it's a woman they know as Ivy."

Grice said: "It's like trying to play chess with a piece missing. We know what this Ivy looks like, but a thousand girls would probably answer the same description."

"Medium height, late twenties, dark-haired, always well dressed, thin features, pleasant voice," Rollison said. "She meets the men in bars, pubs, cinemas, theatres, all kinds of public places, and—"

He broke off, and caught his breath.

Grice said: "That's not exactly new," and then frowned at Rollison's expression, for Rollison looked as if he could not believe whatever had come to his mind. "What on earth's worrying you?" Grice demanded.

Rollison said: "Bill, it can't be. I'm just seeing double. It can't be."

"You may be seeing double. You're certainly talking double Dutch," Grice said. "What—"

"Bill," said Rollison again, in a taut voice. "She sees them in pubs and picture-palaces and all manner of public places. She gives them their orders, and she pays them their salary in cash. What does that remind you of?"

"I can't imagine—" Grice began, and then stopped short, and for a moment his expression was as bewildered as Rollison's.

In fact the Toff began to recover, and began to smile in a curiously twisted way, while staring into Grice's brown eyes as if he were beginning to enjoy the shock effect on Grice.

"No," said Grice, chokily.

"Yes. Marjorie Fryer was murdered after going round from pub to pub, club to club, picture-palace to picture-palace, ostensibly following Bob Benning. Marjorie Fryer had some ready money after her visits, as if she collected a kind of blackmail or was paid a retainer. And Marjorie was murdered. Why, Bill? Because she was hoping to wreck the romance of a nice pair of kids? Or because she had been exerting pressure on our Ivy's boss too long, and she had to be killed? Benning was perfectly placed as the man to take the blame."

"Good God!" gasped Grice, and gulped, and said: "Rolly, it begins to look as if you're right."

"Coincidence would take us so far, but surely no further," said Rollison. He stood up. "Come and see my heat-treatment victim." He led the way into the room where the prisoner was sitting back, sandwiches and tea by his side. "See how well we treat our guests." The man glanced at Grice and back to Rollison. "More questions," Rollison went on, "and you've nothing to fear if you answer off the cuff. Did you know Marjorie Fryer, the girl who was murdered last Monday night?"

There was a long pause before the prisoner said: "Yes, I've known her for months. She found something out about Ivy, and we had to pay her five pounds every week to keep her quiet. But I don't know anything about her murder! I had nothing to do with it, but I—I can't prove it." He was almost shouting. "I was at the Ealing Bank job on Monday, I wasn't in the East End."

Rollison heard him, but did not greatly care whether he was the killer or not.

The "double" was a double indeed; the two cases were now one. But why had both been brought to him? That was the overriding question. He could accept coincidence with any man, but not such a coincidence as this. Why—

A telephone bell rang.

Rollison took Grice's arm.

"Come on," he said, and hurried into the big room, where Jolly was already at the telephone.

Grice had the bewildered look which seldom affected him. Jolly could see the expression of excitement in Rollison's eyes, and stood waiting for the caller, and then said: "It's for you, Mr. Grice."

"Thanks," said Grice, in a gruff voice, as if he were telling himself that he must pull himself together. He strode to the telephone. "Grice here."

He listened.

His eyes began to shine, and when he spoke again it was in a sharper, much more confident voice: "Fine. Get a general call put out for her. Send to all pubs and clubs in the East End and the West End. Don't lose her." He put the receiver down, and turned to Rollison. "A man got a lift in Fred Martin's lorry this afternoon."

"Ah!"

"'He was with a dark-haired young woman, of medium height, who was very well dressed. She had been waiting nearby in a Sunbeam Rapier car, and a police patrol noticed them and saw them get out of the car and walk towards the main road. These policemen saw them hold up Martin's lorry. The man got into the cabin, and the woman went back to her car. The patrol men thought it odd, but didn't know about the accident—they went off duty almost immediately afterwards. They picked up the S.O.S. on the radio to-night, and—"

Grice broke off.

"Wonderful, Bill! It looks as if it's falling right into our hands. All we want is Ivy. Just Ivy. An Ivy who might be interested in framing young Benning, an Ivy who gets around a great deal. She wouldn't use her real name, of course; it would be a false name for her contact work. Ivy. And we want to know why I was called into both

153

cases. Remember your little diatribe on coincidence? For once we're in full agreement. Bill, why—"

He broke off again, and for a moment he looked almost as astounded as he had in the beginning. But this time he recovered more quickly. The light in his eyes was radiant, and it was quite obvious he believed he had come upon the truth.

"There was no danger for Cedric Dwight," he said, softly. "The attack on him was a fake, or we would have found the bullet. It was his way of getting into my flat—because he wanted to find out how much I knew. You and Dwight really had the same delusion—that I knew much more than I did; and the timing of Dwight's coming must have some significance, too—just after Isobel and Mrs. Benning had come to see me. If Dwight was involved in Marjorie Fryer's murder, he would want to know what I was going to do. Being in the flat gave him all he wanted. When he realised that I knew next to nothing, he allowed himself to be kidnapped."

"Rolly—" Grice began.

"That isn't all," Rollison hurried on. "There was pressure to bear on Dwight's wife, but not on him. He seemed terrified, but recovered remarkably soon when I offered to let him stay here. In fact he was happy. I think that we shall find that putting him in the boot of my car was to fool me again. Everything about Cedric Dwight is a fake. His wife was involved in one of the kinds of crimes that Ivy's men have been committing in—Kitty was part of the whole, a cog in the machine. And you can take it that Cedric liked the look of her, fixed that acquaintance, and decided to marry her. Poor, poor, deluded Cedric; always sheltering behind his delusions, always ready with an excuse for any odd things that he did, but brilliantly clever at organising this crime. Do you think that Marjorie Fryer found out that he was involved?"

Rollison was talking in a low-pitched voice, and looking towards the door. Only a few yards away, Cedric Dwight was lying – or sitting up. It was possible that the man was just outside this room.

Listening.

Rollison went on: "Marjorie certainly made some vital discovery and used it too freely. Bill, we've got Dwight right here, and we've got to force an admission out of him."

Then there was a knock at the front door, startling him. That door was through the lounge hall, opposite the door of the passages leading to the other parts of the flat. He heard Jolly's footsteps. He contrasted the normality of that with the astonishing revelation which he felt sure was vital. He heard Jolly open the door, and then heard a young woman say: "I must see Mr. Rollison. I must see him!"

It was Isobel Cole.

Chapter Twenty-Two

Double Complete

"I wonder what the devil she wants now," said Grice, and then saw Rollison smiling at him, and growled: "For once in my life I need a drink, Rolly. Mind if I help myself? I'm used to building cases up step by step; this speed isn't my way of working at all."

"Nice to think I'm becoming appreciated," Rollison said. "Yes, help yourself." He saw the door open wide, and Jolly appear, with the girl just behind him. "All right, Jolly. I'll see Miss Cole," he said, and Jolly stood aside for the girl to hurry across to him.

She looked very beautiful indeed.

Her dark hair was unruly, and her coat was open, with the inside tying tape hanging down. There was even less doubt about her statistics. She had lovely slim legs, too, and as she came to Rollison her hands were outstretched.

"You must come and help me," she said, and took his hands. "Bob's mother is beside herself. She thinks it's because of trying to save Bob that Fred Martin was killed. Someone's told her that you don't think it was an accident, and it's all over the East End that it was murder. You must come and comfort her."

"I wonder," said Rollison, quite unexpectedly.

"Oh, please. You must!"

"Isobel, you couldn't be over-acting, could you?" Rollison asked softly. "You could be a double for Ivy. Or could you?"

She raised one hand, as if astounded. Her make-up was better, her clothes were better, she looked wholly mature – and almost vicious.

Then a sound came at the door. Rollison heard Jolly exclaim, and looked round quickly.

There was Cedric Dwight.

He had a small automatic in his hand.

He looked taller and slender and willowy. His hair was falling low on his forehead and nearly covered one eye. He was moving in slowly, and his wife was just behind him; her breathing was very heavy, as if she were more terrified than ever.

"Don't try any tricks, Toff," Dwight said, and moved to one side. "Come in, Kitty. Jolly, my man"—he actually grinned—"don't try to slip out the other way. Your East End friend is communing with himself in an armchair. I hit him over the head very hard. And my friend and helpmate will do whatever I tell her—won't you, Kitty?"

Kitty said: "Of—of course."

"She dare not do anything else," explained Cedric Dwight. "I have an effect on some women. And Superintendent, it's no use looking as if you wish it were possible to break my neck. It isn't. The man who suffered the heat treatment isn't in a very good mood, by the way."

Rollison was standing by the Trophy Wall, very close to the hangman's noose. Grice was with him, massive, tense, obviously ready to take a chance with Dwight. In the doorway leading to the front door there was Jolly, with the erstwhile prisoner just behind him, carrying a hammer, one kept in the kitchen for domestic purposes. And near Rollison was Isobel Cole, standing quite upright.

"Don't," whispered Rollison to Grice.

"Excellent advice," said Dwight. "Don't move an inch, either of you, or I'll shoot. You—" He motioned to Isobel with the gun in his hand. "Get away from Rollison, get out of his reach. You're the really unlucky one here."

"What do you mean?" demanded Isobel, in a shrill voice. "You wouldn't—"

"If you hadn't chosen to come just now you wouldn't have walked into this trouble. The heat-treatment trouble. My friend Arthur had a bright idea when I freed him just now, Toff. That the heat treatment should be varied a little. We are going to set fire to this flat, with you, Grice, Jolly, and poor Isobel Cole. After all, any wise man would destroy the evidence against him, wouldn't he? And you are deadly evidence against me."

Kitty gasped: "Cedric, you can't—"

"Don't interrupt me, sweetheart," said Cedric Dwight. "I can indeed. There is just one person in this world who knows that I have planned and plotted all this, and who could name me. That's Ivy. My old flame, Ivy!" He laughed on a high-pitched note. He wasn't normal, of course; he never had been normal. "And she is going to vanish, never to reappear. The police won't be able to find her, and therefore won't be able to find me. But Rollison was too clever, and worked it all out by himself. Do you know exactly why it started, Toff?"

"I can guess."

"Guess."

Rollison said: "You once used Marjorie Fryer as you later used your Kitty. That set Marjorie on the downward path. She knew you from the early days of the planning and plotting, and blackmailed you. So you had to have her killed. You were afraid that if I probed too deeply, with the help of Ebbutt's men and the Salvation Army, that I'd get at the truth. You didn't want to risk that, so you started a diversion. It was a mistake, but at the same time it seemed a brilliant idea. You would establish yourself here, find out exactly what I was doing on the other case, and know precisely when to act if danger threatened. Right?"

"The man who died because he was too smart," said Dwight, brightly.

"Cedric—" Kitty began, chokily.

"You can't let this devil do anything to me! You can't!" Isobel cried.

Rollison ignored her, and spoke to Dwight.

"And to keep me busy on an illusory fight, you had your men attack me. You knew that I was likely to get help from Ebbutt, so you had your men stir up the Razzo boys to give Ebbutt plenty to think about. If Ebbutt's men were busy with the Razzo mob, they couldn't do much to help me. So you did everything you could to make sure that I couldn't hope to concentrate on the Benning case— the big weakness in your hand."

"Nice reasoning," approved Dwight. "I almost wish it weren't necessary to—"

Then, Grice moved.

He meant to give Rollison a chance to act, of course, to distract Dwight's attention for a vital second. Almost as he moved, Dwight shot him. Rollison actually heard the thud of the bullet in Grice's chest, heard him gasp, and saw him begin to pivot round. And Dwight was good with a gun. The one shot came, sharp and clear; and then the gun pointed towards Rollison, covering him so that he was in as helpless a position as Grice.

Isobel gave a little, choking cry.

Grice fell, heavily, but he did not lose consciousness. Rollison could see the way he twisted round, hoping that he would win another chance to stop the man with the gun.

"Odds even worse now," said Dwight, cheerfully. "You aren't saying much, Rollison. Don't say that now you're looking in the face of death you don't like the idea. I seem to remember that you've helped to send a lot of people to the gallows, and you've also managed to involve poor innocents, like Fred Martin."

Rollison didn't speak.

Jolly said: "Mr. Rollison, sir—"

"Don't move, Jolly," Rollison ordered. The words were hardly necessary, for the prisoner who had suffered the heat treatment was close enough to grab Jolly's arm; and close enough to smash that hammer down on his head. "Kitty, go and get a towel from the bathroom, and come back and pad the Superintendent's wound."

"It isn't worth the trouble," Cedric Dwight said, and now he was sneering. "Nothing's worth the trouble, Toff. Arthur, fix Jolly, and get that petrol."

Jolly tried to move forward; the man behind him struck a swift and vicious blow, and Jolly pitched forward.

There seemed an awful inevitability about everything that happened, as if it had been willed this way, and that there was nothing that Rollison or anyone else could do about it. Kitty turned away, suddenly, as if she could not face what was happening; she went out of the room.

"If you take it easy," Dwight said to Rollison, "I'll make it better for you. I'll give you a sleeping pill, which works very quickly and you'll be out before the fire starts on you. Little Isobel, too."

"No!" Isobel cried, and swung round on Rollison, flung her arms about his neck and clung to him, holding him tight. "Don't let him do this to me, don't let him do it!"

Panic was in her voice, and it was surprising that there should be such strength in her lovely body.

Dwight was grinning.

The man who had suffered heat treatment was back in the room, carrying a can of petrol which Jolly always had on the premises for cleaning purposes. He unscrewed the cap, and was ready to splash the petrol about. The smell rose from the can, sharp and overpowering. The girl still clung to Rollison, while Grice stared up despairingly, as if pleading with him to make some effort to prevent this awful thing from happening.

"Don't let him!" screeched Isobel. "Stop him; I can't stand it, I just can't stand it!"

"Can't you?" asked Rollison, and quite suddenly slid his arms around her, hugged her very tight, and lifted her high off the ground. He twisted round so that he was between the two men and the door leading to the lounge hall. "Ivy," he said, "you tried very hard, but it didn't work. What is it like to have two names?"

She was rigid in his grasp.

He saw Dwight fire. He dodged. The bullet actually touched the girl's hair. Now she started to kick and bite, but he held her absolutely fast as he backed into the lounge hall. He kicked the door to, but it did not slam. He flung the girl away from him, and as she staggered, snatched open the front door.

There was Wrightson; and behind him, five or six of Ebbutt's men, carrying sticks; one of them actually carried an old Webley revolver.

"He'll try to shoot his way out," Rollison said. "Don't let—"

There was the roar of the old Army gun, and the sharper report of Dwight's automatic. Rollison felt himself thrust out of the way by Wrightson, and as he staggered, saw that Dwight was falling, and that the gun was dropping from his hand.

Ivy-Isobel was screaming.

The man who had suffered the heat treatment was running through the flat, and suddenly there was a roar of voices from the kitchen. Rollison knew that Dwight's man had opened the door to more of Ebbutt's cronies, who were waiting to come in.

"One of the Army girls said she thought Isobel looked remarkably like another woman who visited pubs sometimes," Wrightson said, "and you'd told us to watch Isobel. So when we saw her coming this way, we made up a bigger party. O.K., Mr. Ar?"

Chapter Twenty-Three

All Square

Rollison stepped out of his Rolls-Bentley outside the hospital, was recognised by the porters, the nursing staff, and most of the patients as he walked by some of the wards, for he had been here several times already. He waved and smiled right and left as he hurried through passages filled with the faintly astringent smell of antiseptics. He saw that the door of the Sister's room was open, and tapped.

The Sister looked up, an elderly woman whose eyes brightened at the sight of the Toff.

"Good morning, Mr. Rollison. I'm so glad to tell you that Mr. Grice is much better."

"Wonderful!"

"And Mr. Jolly will be discharged this afternoon, although it is essential that he should take it easy for a week or two. He is a remarkably resilient man for his age, but—"

"He shall have a month in the South of France."

"That's exactly what he needs," said the Sister. "Would you like a nurse to escort you to Mr. Grice's ward?"

"I think I know the way," said Rollison.

It was four days after the raid on his flat, and in those few days he had probed and talked and discovered nearly everything that he now knew about the case of the deadly double. He tapped on Grice's door, heard Grice's "Come in" uttered in a strong voice, went in, and saw the look of expectancy on the Yard man's face turn to one of disappointment.

"Oh, it's you."

"Anyone would think you didn't owe me what's left of your life," said Rollison, mildly.

"Oh, I don't mind seeing you," said Grice, "but I was expecting my wife."

"She telephoned to say she's been held up for half an hour," Rollison told him, "so you'll have to make do with me for the time being. How are you feeling, Bill?"

"I'm fine."

"I'm told you'll be off duty for two months," Rollison said, "and that'll be the first real holiday you've had for fifteen years." He pulled up a chair. "I promised your wife I'd tell you everything, so that you could tell it to her and show her what a wonderful detective you are."

Grice, who looked very pale and whose eyes still held the shadow of great strain, forced a smile.

"You don't improve," he said. "But I always said you were good at guesswork."

"Oh, my dear chap," Rollison protested. "Not guesswork. Sometimes we guess, but now and again something makes four out of two and two even in my mind."

"Prove it."

Rollison leaned back in the chair, pressed the tips of his fingers together professionally, and said earnestly: "Very good, sir. It really began when I first heard of Ivy. You rightly said that her description would fit a thousand girls, and it might have been coincidental that it fitted Isobel Cole. Isobel was pert, pretty, and naïve. Isobel was virtually forced to come to me by Benning's mother. Over the telephone she once tried to put me off the case—but Benning's mother wasn't having any. Isobel was always out three nights a week, at these 'art lessons' she had, but although I didn't have time to check, I was never persuaded that art was her strong suit. The real key was in the fact that Marjorie Fryer was supposed to have threatened that she would tell Isobel Cole about the licentiousness of Robert Benning. Supposing, in fact, Marjorie had also threatened Isobel-Ivy that she would tell Robert Benning what she knew about her. That would make a perfect motive for murdering Marjorie and framing Benning."

"Yes," conceded Grice, after a moment's thought. "Yes, I can see how you came to that conclusion. You could call it deduction, but it wasn't far from a guess."

"Please yourself," said Rollison, and dropped the pretence at earnestness. "That was pretty well it, Bill. Later I arranged for Isobel to be followed. Everyone took it for granted that I thought she was in danger, of course, but in fact I thought she would carry danger with her wherever she went. And she did. She came to my flat because she knew Dwight was back there and wanted to try to make sure he wasn't suspected. She was as cunning as they come, but she didn't expect Dwight to turn on her the moment there was real trouble. Dwight wanted his Kitty, not Ivy-Isobel, who had served his purpose."

"Incidentally," Rollison added, his eyes kindling, "there was another angle which I didn't see clearly at first, but which I'm sure you would have picked up if you'd seen as much of Kitty Dwight as I saw."

"Blarney apart, what was that?"

"Isobel and Kitty were types. Attractive, good figures, dumb-blondish, even though Isobel was a brunette. They had a *naïveté* which was almost too good to be true, and it puzzled me a lot. Why did it attract Dwight? Puzzling over that, I realised that either girl would be likely to attract Cedric. Someone hated Kitty Dwight, and made things as tough for her as they could. Why not a jealous rival? Why not the woman jilted for Kitty? Why not Ivy, in fact—although at the time I didn't think of her as Ivy. I just marvelled that two people with so much in common should be in the two different affairs. So, I was fooled."

"Not for long," admitted Grice, and shifted his position a little. "Rolly, I've never really seen you in action like that before. Your nerve is almost as good as its reputation."

"Either you or I are reforming," Rollison quipped.

"You'll never reform," Grice retorted. "How's Jolly?"

"Coming out to-day."

"You ought seriously to think of retiring him," Grice declared. "It isn't reasonable to expect him to stand the pace much longer."

"I'd like to see me try to retire him before he's ninety," Rollison scoffed. "Anyhow, where would I be without him? Seen anyone from the Yard lately?"

"The Assistant Commissioner looked in this morning," Grice said. "He told me that all the records of the organisation were found at Ivy-Isobel's flat—damn it, you've got me doubling the name now! I still don't understand why she came to you in the first place."

"I've told you, Bill. Ivy-Isobel made it clear that she wouldn't have come if Benning's mother hadn't practically forced her to. She also arranged with Dwight to keep my mind off the Benning job. They nearly did, too, but they crossed too many t's and dotted too many i's. Racket all over, though, including your motor-bike mob."

"That was one of the most widespread groups we've had to deal with," Grice said. "It operated for a long time before we suspected how big it was; before you did, either, if it comes to that."

"We must get our ears closer to the ground," Rollison conceded, and stood up. "Bill, you'd better have ten minutes' rest before your wife comes. Ever paused to think of what would have happened if Ivy hadn't driven the man to stop Martin's lorry?"

"She took too much on herself," Grice agreed, prosily, "but if she hadn't slipped up that way, she would in another. They always do. Incidentally, we didn't have another informer about the passenger in that lorry. You sometimes have the luck."

"Mostly in my friends," Rollison said. "The real red herring was Dwight, of course. He used his childhood delusions wherever they would help."

"Don't rub it in," Grice begged. "And remember he didn't need money; he just got a perverted thrill out of being a big shot. That's one reason why he fooled us at the Yard."

Rollison agreed; shook hands; smiled; and went out.

He strolled more slowly towards the front of the hospital, more preoccupied than when he had come in, although he ignored no one who took the trouble to wave or speak to him. He was glad to get outside. He got into his car and looked up at the hospital, telling himself that he would be coming here on and off for several weeks. Bill Ebbutt wouldn't be out for a month, and Grice would have at least another three weeks.

Rollison found himself thinking about Dwight as he drove back to the West End.

Dwight was in a different hospital, recovering from his wound, and would soon stand trial. Ivy-Isobel hadn't been hurt. The Yard had questioned Kitty, but there was as yet no charge against her, and there wasn't likely to be. These things Rollison knew, and they gave him some cause for satisfaction, but whenever he thought of the case he also thought of the Salvation Army trombonist, of his wife, and of little Mrs. Benning.

Bob Benning was free, of course.

Rollison reached his flat, where Wrightson, wearing striped trousers and a black coat, greeted him with an expansive grin and said as he stepped inside: "Getting as good as Jolly, aren't I?"

"Provided you never tell him so, yes."

"Oh, I wouldn't tell the old cove," said Wrightson. "I don't mind telling you that he's the salt of the earth, Jolly is. The salt of the earth. Like old Bill Ebbutt and Lil. Funny thing, I never used to have much time for Lil," went on Wrightson. "I always thought she was a humbugging old hypocrite with her singing and her blowing and her get-down-on-yer-knees talk. Shows how wrong you can be about people. You heard?"

Rollison was thinking of Fred and his Jane.

"What?"

"They're planning a bang-on concert party and a couple of bouts for the day Bill gets home," said Wrightson. "Getting two or three of the best *artistes*, and you'd never believe, they're going to have an Army band there. How about that? The proceeds will all be devoted to the widow of Fred Martin, too. Salt of the earth, that's what Jolly is."

"*Jolly?*"

"He'd suggested it to me while we was washing up," said Wrightson, simply.

The concert was held five weeks afterwards to the day. There were three bouts at a fast clip, there were five of the West End's leading *artistes* and television favourites. There was the Salvation Army Band, led for the occasion by Lil Ebbutt, who had never stood so straight nor looked with such pride at her Bill.

Bill Ebbutt was at the ringside in a wheel-chair, and his grin had never been more expansive. He had lost weight, he wheezed less, and looked better than Rollison had known for some time.

There was Jane Martin, singing in a clear contralto, and her only son, young Fred, playing the trombone with a gusto which would have done his father's heart good. There was Mrs. Benning, in a ringside seat, and Bob Benning – and with him, Kitty Dwight, looking almost fragile in her beauty.

There was Grice.

And there was Jolly, sitting by Wrightson's side, acting as master of ceremonies.

Every square inch of the gymnasium filled. Outside was a huge crowd of people, listening to the relay of the performance.

And of course, there was the Toff.

"Ladies and gentlemen," boomed Percy Wrightson, a little before half-past ten. "We are nearing the end of our performance, and we hope a good time was had by all. Before we have 'the Queen', though, Mrs. Ebbutt wants a word—our Lil. Give her a hand, boys—*our Lil!*"

They roared—

Lil was helped into the canvas ring, and stood alone, upright in her uniform and wearing her Army bonnet.

"Ladies and gentlemen," she called in her clear and authoritative voice, so often raised at prayer meetings and exhortation to the Godless. "Everyone here knows the real man behind the scenes to-night, Mr. Anonymous as he's known sometimes—when he gives a lot of money to the deserving—and Mr. Ar when he just pops in for a quick one. He doesn't know it, but we've got a little presentation for him to-night. Come on, Mr. Ar Anonymous—step right up."

Rollison, until then thoroughly enjoying himself, was startled and a little wary as he climbed into the ring. Lil shook hands, solemnly. Then the band struck up the old, old song, *For He's A Jolly Good Fellow*. The crowd took it up with throaty gusto which not only made the roof shake, but also made the Toff feel prickly about the eyes.

That came to an end at last, and there was a moment's silence. Then he noticed that Lil was taking off her bonnet. Suddenly she handed it to him, and he knew that everyone here expected this, or they would have been demanding a speech.

"Mr. Ar," said Lil, still firmly, "we all know that you have a Trophy Wall at your flat, and we agreed that you had to have a souvenir of this case. So *here* it is. God bless you as long as you keep it. I know that'll be all your life."

Rollison took the bonnet.

He had never been so touched.

He heard the shouts coming, and warm laughter, and the demand: "Speech!" a man cried. "Speech!" more shouted. "Speech, speech, speech!" a hundred people bellowed. Grice was joining in, Benning and Kitty were joining in, Jolly was joining in. "Speech, Mr. Ar. Speech, Toff. Come on, Toff, give us a speech!"

It was the only time that the Toff could remember being at a loss for words.

JOHN CREASEY

GIDEON'S DAY

Gideon's day is a busy one. He balances family commitments with solving a series of seemingly unrelated crimes from which a plot nonetheless evolves and a mystery is solved.

One of the most senior officers within Scotland Yard, George Gideon's crime solving abilities are in the finest traditions of London's world famous police headquarters. His analytical brain and sense of fairness is respected by colleagues and villains alike.

'The finest of all Scotland Yard series' – New York Times.

GIDEON'S FIRE

Commander George Gideon of Scotland Yard has to deal successively with news of a mass murderer, a depraved maniac, and the deaths of a family in an arson attack on an old building south of the river. This leaves little time for the crisis developing at home ....

'Gideon of Scotland Yard emerges as one of the most real working detectives in modern fiction.... A sympathetic and believable professional policeman.' - New York Times

JOHN CREASEY

THE CREEPERS

"The prisoner's hand was thin and bony ... And in the centre of the palm was a pinkish mark. It was the shape of a wolf's head, mouth open, fangs showing. Although it was what he had expected to see, Inspector West felt a twinge of repugnance a stab not unrelated to fear. It was the fifth time he had seen the mark of the wolf – the mark of Lobo."

A gang of cat burglars led by Lobo cause mayhem as they terrorize the city. They must be stopped, but with little in the way of evidence the police are baffled. Just how can Inspector West manage to do this in what is a race against time before more victims succumb?

"Here is an excellent novel of law enforcement officers, harried, discouraged and desperately fatigued, moving inexorably ahead under the pressure of knowledge that they must succeed to save human lives." - Cleveland Plain-Dealer

"Furiously exciting" - Chicago Tribune

"The action is fast, continuous and exciting" - San Francisco News

JOHN CREASEY

INTRODUCING THE TOFF

Whilst returning home from a cricket match at his father's country home, the Honourable Richard Rollison - alias The Toff - comes across an accident which proves to be a mystery. As he delves deeper into the matter with his usual perseverance and thoroughness , murder and suspense form the backdrop to a fast moving and exciting adventure.

'The Toff has been promoted to a place of honour among amateur detectives.' – *The Times Literary Supplement*

CASE AGAINST PAUL RAEBURN

Chief Inspector Roger West has been watching and waiting for over two years – he is determined to catch Paul Raeburn out. The millionaire racketeer may have made a mistake, following the killing of a small time crook.

Can the ace detective triumph over the evil Raeburn in what are very difficult circumstances? This cannot be assumed as not eveything, it would seem, is as simple as it first appears .....

'Creasey can drive a narrative along like nobody's business ... ingenious plot ... interesting background .' - *The Sunday Times*